"Tell me v

l. "Because ... o lose contr

She saw him swallow, saw the muscles in his jaw clench. "Tell me you want this as much as I want you."

His words, *I want you*, sent another throb through her body. So close. She was poised on the edge of release. Another shifting of his body, another touch of Oz's mouth on her nipple or her neck, and she was going to throw herself into wild abandonment.

She wanted him. She was hungry for him. More than she'd been hungry for anything, since—

Marianne gasped, and stiffened in Oz's embrace.

The last time she'd wanted anything this badly, she'd nearly killed herself for it.

Dear Reader

When I wrote FEATURED ATTRACTION, the hero's best friend, Oz, kept on nagging at me. He came to life in my head and he demanded a book of his own. So I wrote it, because I thought he was a major hottie and I wanted to know what happened to him, too.

When I started writing, I believed that I knew the plot of this story. In particular, I had a definite idea of what was going to happen after Marianne paid a lot of money for a date with Oz and the two of them ended up on a midnight coastline in Maine.

Oz and Marianne both knew what was going to happen, too, I thought.

We were all wrong.

As I was writing the scene, Marianne took over. To her surprise, and to mine, and to Oz's, she flat-out refused to do what I thought she would do. She did something else instead. And throughout the story she kept on surprising me, acting differently than I (and she, and Oz) had planned. A typical bad girl, huh? Except it's not quite like that.

It's great to write stories where the characters spontaneously come to life. I hope you enjoy Oz and Marianne as much I did...even when I was tearing my hair out.

I love to hear from readers. Please e-mail me at julie-cohen@ntlworld.com, or write to me care of Mills & Boon, and visit my website, www.julie-cohen.com.

Julie

Recent titles by Julie Cohen:

FEATURED ATTRACTION

...and look out for Julie Cohen's next book in June 2006:

DELICIOUS

BEING A BAD GIRL

BY
JULIE COHEN

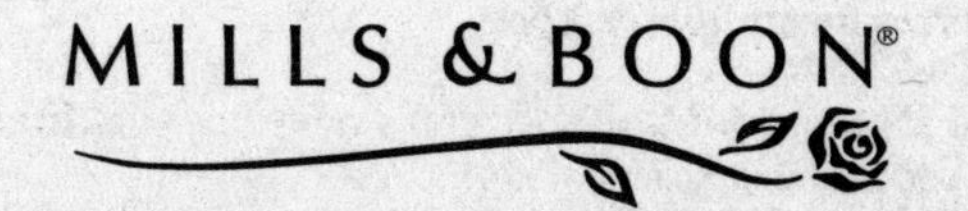

DID YOU PURCHASE THIS BOOK WITHOUT A COVER?

If you did, you should be aware it is **stolen property** as it was reported *unsold and destroyed* by a retailer. Neither the author nor the publisher has received any payment for this book.

All the characters in this book have no existence outside the imagination of the author, and have no relation whatsoever to anyone bearing the same name or names. They are not even distantly inspired by any individual known or unknown to the author, and all the incidents are pure invention.

All Rights Reserved including the right of reproduction in whole or in part in any form. This edition is published by arrangement with Harlequin Enterprises II B.V. The text of this publication or any part thereof may not be reproduced or transmitted in any form or by any means, electronic or mechanical, including photocopying, recording, storage in an information retrieval system, or otherwise, without the written permission of the publisher.

This book is sold subject to the condition that it shall not, by way of trade or otherwise, be lent, resold, hired out or otherwise circulated without the prior consent of the publisher in any form of binding or cover other than that in which it is published and without a similar condition including this condition being imposed on the subsequent purchaser.

MILLS & BOON and MILLS & BOON with the Rose Device are registered trademarks of the publisher.

First published in Great Britain 2006
Harlequin Mills & Boon Limited,
Eton House, 18-24 Paradise Road, Richmond, Surrey TW9 1SR

© Julie Cohen 2006

ISBN 0 263 84986 4

Set in Times Roman 10½ on 12 pt.
171-0406-55780

Printed and bound in Spain
by Litografia Rosés S.A., Barcelona

For Anna, Biddy, Jenny, Kathy and Tanya, all of whom wanted to fight Marianne for Oz.

Thanks for motorcycle information to John Levesque of 'Harleys R Us' in Lewiston, Maine; Sherry Jones and her descent into biker hell; and Stephen Bowden for the ride down the M4 at 100 mph.

CHAPTER ONE

"OKAY, let me get this straight. Tequila, then salt, then—" Marianne stood, container of salt poised over the cocktail shaker.

"No!" Warren hurled himself across the bar and grabbed her hand. "No salt in the margarita! You put it on the rim of the glass!"

Marianne's hand, jogged by Warren, shook a dollop of rock salt into the container. She looked down into the aluminum cylinder, and an expression of wild regret passed over her face. Then she shook her head a little, and smiled.

"I think salty tequila could be good." She raised the container to her lips, took the tiniest of sips, and grimaced. "Yeah, it's a taste sensation."

Warren laughed. "Hon, you are going to take one load of training before you're good enough to be a bartender."

Marianne dumped the salty booze into the sink, then rinsed out the shaker. "Give me a break, Warren. I only got here yesterday. I'll try again."

She poured another measure of tequila into the shaker. "Okay, no salt. What next?"

Her cousin propped one lean hip against the bar, apparently reassured for the moment that Marianne wasn't going to ruin his entire liquor supply. "Triple sec. Just a shake."

Marianne had to search for several minutes before she found the bottle of orange liqueur. She held the neck of the bottle gingerly above the cocktail shaker, and shook it.

The cap fell off, hitting the aluminum with a hollow thunk, and a waterfall of triple sec poured into the tequila.

"Marianne!"

Warren's handsome face was the picture of comic outrage. Marianne glimpsed it and in moments she was doubled up against the bar, laughing so hard that tears squeezed from her eyes.

"Who—you—" gasped Warren. He caught his breath, and tried again. "It's a good thing I know that you have an MBA from one of the most prestigious universities in the country, cuz. Because anybody else watching you fail to make this margarita would assume that you were just plain stupid."

"They didn't teach me to mix drinks in business school," Marianne said. She pushed back the strands of her dark hair that had escaped her ponytail.

"You're telling me." Warren took the shaker from her and sniffed it. "I don't guess you did much partying at college, huh, Goody Two-shoes?"

"That's why I have to make up for it now." She grinned at Warren.

Warren dumped out the overly orangefied tequila, and then he leaned on the glossy bar and looked straight into Marianne's face.

"Hon, you know my tequila is yours to ruin. But I have to say it was a surprise to see you."

Marianne filled herself a glass of water, assessing how much to tell her cousin.

"You've got everything in Webb," he continued. "You're practically the town princess. Webb High valedictorian. Webb County Cotton Queen just like your mama, what, two years in a row?"

"Three."

"Three. You're even prettier than I thought. MBA from Duke just like your daddy. Best-looking fiancé in the state, from what I've heard. And an executive job at Webb Enterprises. You've got the whole town of Webb at your feet. Hell, you've got the whole state of South Carolina at your feet. Why'd you suddenly come up here to Maine and learn how to make margaritas?"

Marianne sighed. "I'm sick of being Marianne Webb."

And being Marianne Webb had made her sick, too, but Marianne wasn't going to talk about how she'd pressured herself into an eating disorder, trying to make herself even more perfect. That was over now.

"I want a chance just to be nobody, Warren. An anonymous bartender in a strange town."

She drained the cool water and put down the glass with a bang.

"And I want to have fun. For once. I want to do things just for the heck of it. I want to let down my hair and dance and not worry about what people are going to say about me tomorrow. I want to stay up and see the sun rise and then sleep till noon. I want to go swimming naked and drive too fast and take up with inappropriate men. I *especially* want to take up with inappropriate men."

"So I take it that your engagement to Mr. Perfect is over?"

She laughed, short and sharp and derisive. "My engagement to Jason couldn't be more over."

"What happened with him? I thought you two were like Barbie and Ken."

Ken was actually not a bad description of Jason, now that she thought about it. A perfect, inflexible doll with a painted-on smile.

"Jason liked the fact that I was successful and a former beauty queen and a Webb. He really liked the fact that my daddy is the richest man in town. He liked that we looked good together, and he liked the idea that we were going to have a bunch of good-looking children. He didn't love me, though. He just loved everything that came with me."

That used to come with me, Marianne added mentally.

"I'm sorry, hon," Warren said. "From your e-mails you sounded like you were so sure about him. I was hoping you'd found Mr. Right."

Marianne shook her head. "I thought that Jason was the type of man I should marry. But I didn't love him, any more than he did me. I was trying to convince myself that I did because he was so perfect. I haven't got a broken heart, and I'm not on the rebound. I just want to let loose for a while."

"So," said Warren, "what you're telling me is that Goody Two-shoes Marianne Webb packed her bags two days ago and drove up here to become a born-again bad girl."

"You got it."

"Well. You picked a good night to do it. I'm not sure how inappropriate they'll be, but there'll be a lot of available men in here in about an hour and a half. We've got a charity bachelor auction here tonight."

"That sounds wild." Marianne felt a smile touch her lips. She wasn't certain whether it was a devilish smile or not, but it sure felt like one.

It also felt good.

"Are you going to bid?" she asked.

He shook his head. "They're bound to all be straight. Which is a shame. Still, I'm not complaining. In an hour this place is going to be packed with women bidding for bachelors. It's going to be too busy for your first night. So you can just help collect glasses and things, get a feel for the place, all right?"

"I can work behind the bar," Marianne protested. She grabbed the half-empty triple-sec bottle, hid it behind her back, and flashed a dazzling smile at Warren.

"Honey, I believe you can do whatever you set your mind to do. But tonight you just collect glasses, 'kay? Break yourself in easy. Leave my booze supply alone for a while." Warren winked. "Besides, you might see yourself a bachelor you want to bid on."

"What do you bid for? A date?"

"I think it's a date. But once the money changes hands you and the bachelor can make up the rules yourself." The phone rang out back, and Warren went to answer it.

Make up the rules yourself, mused Marianne. After years of having the rules made up for her, that sounded exactly like what she was looking for.

A born-again bad girl would need a bad bachelor. Someone wild, and reckless, and sexy as sin. Someone who didn't follow any rules but his own.

Marianne smiled. As if she'd know what a bad boy was like unless one came up and bit her on the behind.

She poured a splash of tequila into an empty glass

and held it up to an imaginary bad boy. "To bites on the behind," she said, and poured the liquor into her mouth.

And immediately coughed it out.

"I can't believe I let you talk me into selling my body on the open market," Oz said.

He looked at his reflection in Jack's living-room mirror. He was wearing enough leather to upholster a sofa. Okay, the jacket was his, and that wasn't bad. And although the boots were covered in studs and chains, he was sure they had a certain appeal for some people.

Sadomasochists, for example.

But between the jacket and the boots he was wearing…chaps.

Black leather, zipped and snapped up the sides of both his legs, and buckled around his waist, beneath the black Harley Davidson T-shirt that Jack had given him earlier.

"I think the chaps are overdoing it a little," Oz said.

"They're perfect," Jack assured him. "Chicks dig that stuff."

"Well, you're the expert," Oz allowed.

"I'm only an expert on Kitty nowadays," Jack corrected him. "And Kitty will tell you I'm right." He stepped back and assessed Oz. "Except for one thing. Take off your jacket and your T-shirt."

Oz shook his head. "No way, buddy. No way. I'm drawing the line. I did not suffer through nine years of university education so I could prostitute myself naked on a stage."

"Relax," said Jack. "I'm not going to make you go to the bachelor auction naked. Though you'd probably make a lot more money for the charity if you did," he added.

"Just give me your shirt. And remember, this is all for the youth center. It's a good cause. I'd be out there semi-naked myself, if I weren't extremely happily married."

Oz sighed and shucked off his jacket and pulled off his shirt. "I honestly do not see how this is going to work," he said, handing them over to Jack. "Nobody's going to believe that I usually wear chaps."

"Of course not," said Jack. "Portland's a small city. Most of the women in that room are going to know that you're Dr. Oscar Strummer, clinical psychologist, university lecturer, and eligible bachelor. But you're giving them an extra fantasy to buy."

With a quick movement of his arms, Jack ripped one sleeve off the T-shirt, and then the other. "There. Now wear this. You'll look like Oz, motorcycle rider and hell-raiser. I'm telling you, the bidding will go through the roof. Every woman wants someone who's intelligent and responsible, but who's not afraid to walk on the wild side."

Oz took the shirt from Jack and pulled it back over his head, poking his arms through the frayed holes.

"Wow," came a voice from the doorway. Oz turned to see Jack's wife Kitty, tossing back her vivid red hair and staring at him.

Oz glanced down at himself. Yup, still wearing chaps. "You like this outfit?" he asked.

Kitty nodded once, emphatically. "Oh, yeah. You look good. I'd bid for you."

"See?" Jack said, triumphant. "I told you chicks dig that stuff." He took Kitty's hand and drew her to him. "You better not dig Oz too much, though, sweetheart."

Kitty, nestled in the crook of her husband's arm, smiled up at him and kissed the side of his jaw. "You could get a pair of chaps, Jack. I think that *Easy Rider* look would suit you."

Oz looked away from his embracing friends and studied his leather-clad figure in the mirror. He tried to tug his messy blond hair into some sort of order, but it wasn't cooperating. As usual.

You're too grown-up and well-adjusted to feel jealous of your best friend, he told himself silently.

Jack Taylor, who'd never wanted to get married, had met the woman of his dreams. And Oscar Strummer, who'd always wanted a happy marriage, somebody who belonged to him, hadn't met anybody who even came close.

"You'd think having a Ph.D. in psychology would give me some control over my own psyche," Oz muttered, and adjusted his chaps. The things made him look as if his butt and crotch were hanging out, even though he was wearing faded jeans underneath them.

"Forget the Ph.D." Jack came up behind him and clapped him on the shoulder. "Tonight, you're a sex object to dozens of women. Maybe hundreds. Relax and enjoy."

"But first, give me your arm." Oz felt Kitty tugging on his wrist, and he looked down to see that she was holding a large sponge in one hand.

"This won't hurt a bit," she said, and pressed what looked like a sheet of paper against his upper arm. She swabbed at it with the wet sponge.

"Is that a temporary tattoo?" Oz asked. He might as well be resigned to looking like a Hell's Angel, at least for tonight.

"That's right. You're going to look fantastic."

"I don't think I've worn a fake tattoo since Jack and

I were juniors in high school and we put them on to look older so we could try to buy beer."

Kitty shook her head, still dabbing the sponge. "Girls wear makeup to look older, boys wear fake tattoos, I guess. Were you able to buy the beer?"

"Not a chance. I was sixteen but I still looked twelve, even with the tattoo." Oz chuckled. "I had to be the geekiest kid at Portland High."

"Well." Kitty carefully peeled off the tattoo's backing and admired her handiwork. His biceps were bisected by a large sword with a snake twining around it.

Two blatant phallic symbols. Jack and Kitty weren't being subtle in the least.

"You're certainly not a geek anymore. Nor do you look twelve years old." She grinned up at him. "What are you, six foot three?"

"Four, in these boots, probably."

"You're going to look great on the bike," she said.

Oz narrowed his eyes at her. "What bike?"

Jack was grinning. "C'mon outside, my leather-clad friend."

They wouldn't possibly... Oz followed his friends out of their front door and down their front steps.

Parked on the road outside, gleaming under the streetlight, was a flame-colored, chrome-girdled Harley Davidson motorcycle.

They had.

For a moment, Oz savored the sight of the motorcycle. He imagined it thrumming under his hands, the satisfying roar it would make when he revved the throttle, the feeling of the road rushing under the wheels.

Then real life and responsibility came back to him.

He was a respected clinician and on the teaching staff of the local university.

"I'm not riding a Harley," Oz said.

Kitty skipped ahead of him and stroked her hand against the chrome handlebars. "It's beautiful, isn't it? My brother Nick lent it to us for the weekend. It's his pride and joy. And it's fast, too."

The truth dawned on Oz. For an intelligent guy, he'd been slow on the uptake.

The T-shirt. The boots. The tattoo. The chaps. And now the bike. You didn't just pick this stuff up on your way home from work.

He turned to Jack. "You've been planning this for a long time, haven't you?"

Jack raised his hands in a "what-can-I-say?" gesture. "It's for your own good, Oz. You need a woman in your life. You can't think I haven't noticed that you haven't dated anybody for nearly a year."

"I've had my nineteen-year-old sister living with me," Oz protested. "I haven't exactly been living in a bachelor pad. And since she's moved out I haven't had time for dating. I've taken on more lecturing at the university, on top of the time I commit to my patients."

Kitty laid a gentle hand on his arm. "I think that's part of the problem, Oz. You work too hard. You work all the time." She lowered her voice. "We're worried about you."

Well, of course he worked a lot, Oz thought.

It was a classic displacement strategy. He felt a lack of something in one area of his life, so he made up for it by channelling all of his energy into another area where he was successful. Relationships were non-existent. Work was rewarding.

He knew he was doing it. He knew *why* he was doing it.

But the knowledge didn't seem enough to prevent it happening.

Jack was standing beside him. "C'mon, buddy. I guarantee that if you drive up to the bachelor auction in this getup, you will have at least five women's phone numbers before you even take the keys out of the ignition. And one of those women will even pay good money to go on a date with you. Good money that's going to a good cause."

He nudged Oz with his elbow. "We want you to have some fun. Find a woman and go on a few dates. Maybe even—" he lowered his voice to a conspiratorial whisper "—have sex."

Oz looked at his friends, and the concern in their eyes. Then he looked at the Harley.

Freedom on two wheels.

It wasn't the solution to his problems. He knew better than that. But it was a good escape from them, for a few hours.

He walked across the lawn and threw his leg over the seat of the motorcycle. The leather molded to the shape of his body immediately. The throttle felt as if it belonged in his right hand.

"I haven't been on a motorcycle in eight years," he said, but it was more a statement of fact than a protest.

"They say it's like riding a bicycle," Jack said. "Except a whole lot faster."

Kitty handed him the keys.

The Harley leapt to life beneath him.

He touched the throttle and the world rushed forward.

Oz waved back over his shoulder to his friends. Jack was right about one thing at least. At a bachelor auction, he was guaranteed to end up with a woman at the end of the night.

He wondered what kind of woman she would be.

The room was heaving.

Marianne pushed her way back to the bar, put down her tray of empty glasses, and wiped her forehead with her arm. She was only wearing jeans, sandals, and a sleeveless cotton blouse, but there was a lot of body heat in Warren's bar tonight, and people in Maine didn't seem to believe in air-conditioning in October.

But, darn it, it was *fun.*

About half a dozen bachelors had been auctioned off already. To the best of Marianne's knowledge, there'd been a lawyer, a lobster fisherman, a salesman, a mechanic, a teacher, and an electrician.

Each one of them had come on stage to his own burst of music, and walked up and down the stage, pausing so the audience of women could get a look at him, while the director of the youth center, a sparky woman in her fifties, announced the bachelor's name, his job, where he was from, and other vital statistics.

A couple of them were cute. Most of them were average-looking. This wasn't a celebrity bachelor auction—it seemed to be all local people who wanted to do something for charity. But the men's looks didn't seem to matter. Tonight, every bachelor was eligible.

Each time a man walked on stage, there was a huge feminine cheer from the audience. Wolf whistles, applause, a lot of laughter, and then a room full of women trying to outdo each other.

It wasn't decorous. It wasn't well-bred, or polite, or concerned with keeping up appearances.

Nobody took it too seriously, least of all the bachelors. But underneath the good humor and fun there was an undercurrent of heat that was contributing to the stifling atmosphere in the bar. More than once or twice as she collected glasses and wiped tables Marianne noticed a gleam in a bidding woman's eye that wasn't just from the thrill of the chase. It was plain old desire. The woman was bidding for a date, but underneath she was hoping for more.

And that was more than fun. That was exciting.

Marianne slipped behind the bar and poured herself a glass of water. She fanned herself with her hand and looked around Warren's bar. She'd never seen it before yesterday, but it looked exactly as she would have pictured it. Even as a kid, her cousin had collected interesting items—lawn ornaments, strangely shaped pottery, retro artwork. His bar was bright, cheerful, funky, full of eclectic decorations and relics from Warren's years of club DJing in New York.

Drums and guitars blared from the loudspeakers. A new song for a new bachelor. Marianne recognized it at once: "Born to be Wild."

A perfect song for her mood. She looked up, a smile on her lips, to see what this bachelor was like.

Except there wasn't a bachelor on stage.

The room stilled in anticipation. The only sound was the rock guitars. The heavy bass of the song pounded in Marianne's chest like a second heartbeat.

And then there was another sound: the loud revving of an engine. With a roar, the most extraordinary sight Marianne had ever seen exploded onto the stage.

The motorcycle was a blur, a flash of red and silver. Marianne hardly noticed it. What she saw was the man.

He was big, and tall, and strong. He wore a sleeveless black T-shirt that exposed the muscles of his arms. On the golden skin of one of them, she glimpsed a tattoo. She couldn't tell exactly from here, but his hands looked big enough to wrap around her waist and meet on either side.

At the thought of it, her mouth went dry, even though she'd just drunk a glass of water.

His hair was blond. Streaks of it looked as if they'd been bleached nearly white by the sun. It wasn't that long for a biker's; it didn't reach his collar. But it was wild. As if the wind belonged in it.

"After that entrance, ladies, Oz needs no introduction," said the auctioneer. "Who'd like to start the bidding for our biker boy? Do I hear eighty dollars?"

A forest of hands went up in the audience, and the biker boy smiled. He had a wide mouth, full lips, white, even teeth, and he looked like he smiled a lot.

"Gosh, you are beautiful," Marianne whispered. She'd stopped fanning herself; she was standing stock-still, gripping the bar with both hands, staring and trying to work out what color his eyes were from across the crowded room.

"A hundred dollars to the lady in blue, and do I hear a hundred and twenty? Good, one-twenty to you by the jukebox; will anybody give me one-fifty?"

His name was Oz, she'd said. Oz was a good name for a biker, Marianne thought. A wizard on a motorcycle.

And a wizard in bed?

The thought made her catch her breath.

His long legs were encased in black leather. Marianne imagined how the leather would smell. How it would be warm from him. How, when he stood up from the bike, it would fit the contours of his body.

And what a spectacular body. Even his muscles had muscles. He was one hundred percent male, from his blond hair to his leather-booted toes. Testosterone-ridden.

Dangerous.

"And that's two hundred and fifty dollars. Girls, that's the highest bid we've had so far this evening—let's go as high as we can. It's all for charity. And a date with Oz, of course. Who'll give me three hundred dollars?"

Hands were still waving, blocking her vision of the man on stage. She stood on tiptoe so she could see better.

That wasn't enough. There were still arms waving around everywhere. The bidding seemed to be reaching some sort of a frenzy.

Marianne planted her hands on the bar and hoisted herself up onto it. She scrambled onto her knees on the slippery polished wood.

There. A clear view at last. Clear enough to see his tattoo: a sword and a snake. And that he wasn't wearing leather pants; he was wearing chaps. The black leather framed and drew attention to his crotch, covered in snug faded denim, straddling the flaming red motorcycle.

This man wouldn't be polite. He wouldn't worry about rules. He would do exactly what he wanted, and forget the consequences.

This man was the baddest bad boy she'd ever seen in her life.

He noticed that she was kneeling on the bar watching him. He caught her eye and smiled. And revved the motor of his bike.

The sight of his smile bolted through her like a bullet, and Marianne knew in that moment that he was exactly what she'd left home to look for.

Marianne stood up on the bar. She raised her hand above her head, and raised her voice so it would carry all the way to the stage, and him.

"Three thousand dollars," she yelled.

And then she jumped off the bar and pushed through the crowd to claim her man.

CHAPTER TWO

SHE was sweating, and she wasn't sure whether it was from the heat of the room or from the idea of him. By the time she reached the stage, Marianne's bare arms and shoulders and collarbone were covered in a fine sheen.

About halfway across the room, she'd noticed that everybody was applauding her. A few women held out their hands for her to shake on her way; maybe there were more than a few, but she didn't see them. She was too busy watching her bad boy get off his bike and walk to the edge of the stage. Waiting for her, with a huge smile on his gorgeous face.

The stage wasn't that high, only raised about three feet from the bar's floor, but standing on it the man looked like a giant. He bent down and held out his hands to her. She took them and her heart felt as if it skipped a beat when he lifted her through the air, up to the stage. She landed on her feet, her hands still in his.

"Hi," he said. His voice was deep and warmed by that big white smile. "I'm Oz."

"Hi. I'm Marianne."

He squeezed her hands. "They're all cheering for you, Marianne."

"Are they?" She thought about glancing around at the audience, but she couldn't tear her eyes away from his face.

"They are." With a sudden, fluid movement, Oz let go of her hands and scooped her up into his arms. He held her high up on his chest and her arms instinctively went around his neck. One of his arms cradled her legs; the other held her upper body, his hand resting on her ribs below her breasts. Her cheek was close to the bare skin of his shoulder.

Marianne wanted to stick out her tongue and taste it.

"Go ahead and wave," he told her. His face was so close she could smell toothpaste on his breath when he spoke. He was freshly shaven, too.

She was surprised, and then she didn't know why she was. There was no reason why bikers couldn't own toothbrushes and razors.

She waved one of her arms, keeping the other curled around his neck. The cheers got louder.

"Why's everybody applauding?" she asked, not because she cared, but because his proximity seemed to steal all her wits.

"You just stood on the bar and shouted out a bid that was ten times the going price," he answered. "I think they're impressed."

"Are you?"

He looked into her face. *His eyes are hazel,* she thought dazedly. She hadn't expected that either. She'd expected devilish black, or wolfish blue.

"I'm very impressed," he said.

Good grief, she wanted to kiss the man. And she'd only known him five minutes.

No, wait, scratch that. She didn't know him at all.

And she still wanted to kiss him so badly that she had to bite her lip to stop herself.

He kissed her instead.

His lips pressed onto hers, firm and soft, a total surprise that felt completely right. Marianne's eyes fluttered shut and her arms tightened around his neck. His mouth lingered, and she heard him taking in a long, deep breath through his nose. Inhaling her.

When he let the breath out, she felt the warm air against her cheek, and heard, low in the back of his throat, the quietest of rumbles. A soft moan of pleasure and desire.

Her heart leapt, her ears rang, her head was filled with a thousand voices shouting, "Yes!"

And then he withdrew his mouth from hers, and she blinked at him, and she realized that it wasn't just her head that was full of voices—the whole barroom was erupting with cheers.

He'd just swept a complete stranger up into his arms and kissed her in front of a room full of applauding women.

And it was the best thing he'd done in a very long time. Even better than riding the Harley Davidson, and that was saying something, because the Harley was one incredible machine.

But this woman left the Harley behind in a cloud of dust.

She was beautiful. Slim, leggy, with dark brown hair that was escaping her ponytail in glossy strands around her face. She wore jeans that outlined every curve of her hips and legs, and a white cotton top that clung to her small breasts and exposed a graceful expanse of collarbone and shoulder.

Glancing down, he could see a couple of inches down the front of her shirt, and glimpse the lacy bra beneath it. He felt his breath hitch in his throat.

As soon as she'd knelt on the bar, he hadn't been able to look away from her. She was good-looking enough to be a model or an actress, and she had the elegant posture of a dancer. But what really caught his attention was her skin. It was clear, and soft-looking, and... pure.

With her this close to him, he could see just how perfect it was. Her chest was glossed with perspiration, and her cheeks were flushed and nearly as bright as her blue eyes. And her skin was flawless, creamy and soft, and scented with a powdery, feminine perfume. He'd been able to smell it when he'd kissed her. He inhaled again, and felt as if he were kissing her again.

And this exquisite creature had paid three thousand dollars for *him*? And when he'd kissed her, she'd kissed him back?

More than kissed him back. She'd tightened her arms and arched her body against him.

"I'm a little stunned," he said to her.

"I'm completely stunned," she murmured. She had a soft, slow accent. Her voice hooked him somewhere in his chest. Made it harder to breathe the hot air.

She smiled at him. Two perfect dimples formed in her perfect cheeks.

He was seized by an irrational impulse to kiss her again in front of all these people. And he realized that another irrational impulse was making itself felt in his jeans.

Damn. He was standing in front of a crowd of women, holding a totally stunning stranger in his arms, and he had a boner the size of Los Angeles.

Oz turned and walked back to the Harley. Gently, he set Marianne on the back of the bike. He felt the soft pressure of her arms around his neck even after she'd let him go.

He straddled the idling bike in front of her, and with a touch of the throttle he started the bike forward, and slowly steered them off the stage. He heard a final cheer as they left.

Around the back, there was a set of double doors that led outside to the parking lot. He maneuvered the bike carefully toward them. Oz felt the cooler air hit his face and bare arms as they left the building.

The heat in his veins and between his legs didn't seem to be abating, though. There was no way he could possibly be smelling Marianne's scent, with her behind him, and the cool evening air blowing against his face. But he swore he could still smell her anyway.

Temporary madness? An olfactory hallucination?

Oz shook his head. What was going on here? He'd barely said half a dozen words to this woman.

He turned off the engine. He put down the kickstand, and then got off the bike and held out his hand to help her off. Her hand felt tiny in his.

It was very quiet out here, lit only by a single street-light. Oz was acutely aware that he still had an erection, and that he had absolutely no idea of what to say next.

"It's nice to meet you, Marianne," he said.

Nice to meet you. Pathetic. Nobody would ever know he talked for a living.

"I'm very glad I met you, Oz." Those dimples again, and that accent.

"You're not from around here, are you?" he asked.

"I just got in yesterday. How'd you know?"

"Your accent. You sound like Scarlett O'Hara."

And she looked a little like her, too, with her glossy dark hair and her bright eyes. She put her hands on her hips and stuck out her bottom lip a little, and the resemblance intensified.

"And you are a typical Yankee. *Gone With the Wind* was set in Georgia. I'm from South Carolina. We sound completely different."

"I see." He smiled at her mock rancor. "I guess if somebody said I sounded like I came from Boston, I'd be offended, too."

"I don't know what people in Boston sound like, but Mainers sound funny to me. 'Lobstah.' 'Scahlett.' It's like y'all have got a thing against the letter 'r.'"

"We don't have anything against it. We like it so much we save it for special occasions."

"Well." She tilted her head and looked up at him. She was tall, but the top of her head didn't come much past his chin. "I think this is a special occasion, don't you?"

"I think it is." He formed his mouth into an exaggerated pucker. "Rrrrrrrrrrrrrrrrrrrrrrrrr," he said.

She laughed. It was a deep, throaty sound. A dirty laugh.

It made Oz immediately think about how she would sound moaning with pleasure as he touched her. He imagined his hands running up the insides of her naked pale thighs, and, in his head, he heard her gasp and groan.

Right. Both olfactory and auditory hallucinations. To say nothing of this obsessive need to imagine himself in sexual situations with her. He was going crazy, all right.

And it was the best he'd ever felt.

"How do you like it here?" he asked.

"I like it."

He watched her gaze drop from his face and travel down his body. When she got to his crotch, her eyes widened, and he felt his erection pulse and grow even harder as he realized she could see exactly how much he liked her. Damn chaps framed the thing like an oil painting.

Her eyes lifted back to his face, and he saw her perfect skin was flushed again. She stepped closer to him. Close enough so his nostrils were filled with her scent again, and he could feel the warmth of her body. The tips of her breasts were a bare inch from his chest.

"I like it a lot," she said.

It was a clear invitation for him to do exactly what he wanted. Which was to tangle his hand in her hair, tip her head back, and kiss her again. This time, open-mouthed and hungry. Filling his mouth with her taste, as his head was full of her scent. And to slide the other hand up underneath her vest, touching her perfect skin, making it his.

He lifted his hand to her hair. And then dropped it.

His body desired her. And she evidently desired him. But they were more than bodies.

"You just got into Portland yesterday," he said. "You don't know anything about me."

Her smile was teasing. "I know I like your Harley," she said. "And I know I like the way you look." She touched the side of his leg, lightly caressing the leather of his chaps. "And I know I like you enough to pay three thousand dollars for a date with you."

Borrowed bike. Borrowed clothes. She liked all the things about him that weren't really him. Oz had been right to hesitate before taking their physical relationship any further. He took a step back.

"I don't think that's enough, do you?"

"Three thousand dollars isn't enough for a date?" Her forehead creased.

"Liking my bike and my appearance isn't enough for you to know you want to get involved with me," he said. Telling himself, inwardly, to listen to his own words.

Liking her dimples, her laugh, her accent, her elegance and her perfect, flawless, adorable skin wasn't enough for him to know he wanted to get involved with her. It wasn't enough to base a relationship on.

Of course, he also liked her legs, and her kiss, and her lively blue eyes, and her hair, and her recklessness in standing up on a bar and bidding for him, and her generosity in giving three thousand dollars to charity.

But that wasn't enough either.

Maybe he could learn some more about her and make it enough.

"What are you doing in Portland?" he asked.

She pushed back some strands of hair that had escaped her short ponytail. "I'm working behind the bar at Warren's," she said, "and looking for someone a lot like you. Even though—" she gestured toward him to acknowledge his words "—I don't know you very well. Yet."

"And why are you looking for someone a lot like me?"

The look on her face stole his breath again. She didn't move any closer to him but the air seemed to get thicker, hotter.

"I'm looking for a fantasy," she said. "And I think you can give it to me."

Zoom!

There it went. His libido. His superego, his conscience, his better nature, whatever you wanted to call it, was standing guard trying to keep the naughty guy safely under control and what did his libido do? Cruise straight past the guard, going so fast there was no way of catching him.

His penis wasn't the only thing that was hard at her words. Every muscle in his body tensed, his fingers curling into fists with the strain of not touching her and making her fantasy, whatever it was, come true right now.

"What sort of fantasy would that be?" he asked, rigid all over, trying to keep his voice detached and failing. It sounded gravelly to his own ears.

She seemed to be thinking, though Oz had the distinct impression that she already knew exactly what she wanted to say.

"Well, first, Oz," she said, "I'd like you to take me for a ride on your Harley. I've never been on the back of a bike before."

"And afterward?"

"And afterward, we'll do whatever we feel like doing." Her blue eyes were steady on his. The yellow streetlight gleamed in them.

And then she winked. It was the sexiest thing he'd ever seen.

A date does not consist of ravishing a woman you've just met in the parking lot behind a bar.

"For an investment of three thousand dollars, I should take you to an expensive restaurant and sweep you off your feet," Oz said. He wondered which expensive restaurants in Portland would welcome a woman in jeans and sandals and a man in chaps with a fake tattoo, at ten o'clock at night.

She raised one of her hands and just touched the Harley Davidson logo on his chest. "I think you've already swept me off my feet," she said.

Twice. He'd picked her up twice. And he wanted to pick her up again. Somehow, she felt natural in his arms.

"You really like the motorcycle stuff, don't you?" he asked.

She nodded. "There's just something so—*bad boy* about it."

Bad boy. She thought he was a motorcycle rebel.

Oz ran his hand through his untameable hair—worse for his ride on the Harley. He wasn't a bad boy. Not by any stretch of the imagination.

"Marianne," he said, "there's something you should know."

There must've been something in the way he said it, because her eyelids narrowed just a little, and she swayed just the tiniest bit back. She looked almost as if she were in pain, or desperate.

"Don't," she said.

"Don't what?"

"Don't tell me what I should know. Please. Take me for a ride on your motorcycle. Let me live the fantasy, for once. Let me let go."

Her voice was still strong and confident and tantalizingly sweet. But there was a pleading note, something darker that immediately grabbed him with both hands.

"It's late," he said.

"It's not that late. We've got all night."

All night. For her fantasy.

And, maybe, for his.

He kept telling his patients that fantasies were a normal, healthy way of expressing their desires and if they didn't hurt anybody, there wasn't any harm in trying to act them out.

It could be a revelation. It could be a freedom.

Who was going to get hurt, after all?

"All right," he said. He swept his eyes up and down her body, taking in her pink toes in her sandals, her jeans, her cotton blouse. Her nipples stood out through the thin material, and he didn't think it was just the coolness of the October night air.

"Before you get on the bike, you need to change into shoes. Something sturdy. And you need to wear a jacket, because it'll be cold."

Her smile dug the dimples in her cheeks and nearly blinded him. "Okay."

"I'll meet you out front in ten minutes."

Marianne stood on her tiptoes and kissed him swiftly on the cheek. "Thank you," she said, and then she was gone.

Oz raised his hand to where she'd kissed him. A sweet, innocent, trusting gesture after all of her sexy, seductive words.

He wondered which one was his fantasy: the sexy, knowing Marianne who wanted a bad boy. Or the sweet, somehow desperate Marianne who, miraculously, trusted him enough to let her let go.

CHAPTER THREE

MARIANNE ran up the back stairs. Warren had offered her the spare room of his condo, but she'd said she preferred the independence of living in the disused one-bedroom apartment above the bar.

Her hands were shaking as she unlocked the door and turned the handle.

This is it, she thought. *I'm really doing it. For once, I'm doing what I want, just for me.*

She raced across the bare floorboards of the apartment, dropped to her knees beside the rickety bed, and pulled out her suitcase. The envelope of cash was in one of the inside pockets. Quickly, trembling, she counted it.

"Twenty-four dollars short." She sighed, sinking back on her heels. She'd taken a load of cash out of her checking account before she'd left Webb, but she must've spent more money than she'd thought driving up here.

Two thousand, nine hundred and seventy-six dollars. It was quite a bit of cash to have stowed underneath your bed, in this age of electronic banking.

But not enough for a date with Oz.

Of course, she had checks, a cash card, a savings account and a purse full of credit cards that she didn't want to use. It would be too easy to trace where she was from her statements, and she didn't want her family to find her, just yet.

"Imagine that," she muttered to herself. "The richest little girl in Webb County doesn't have enough money to buy a man."

She stood abruptly and pulled open a drawer in the bureau next to her bed. She found a sweater, and then kicked off her sandals and squashed her feet into a pair of sneakers. She slammed the apartment door behind her and ran down the stairs and through the corridor into the barroom.

The bachelor auction was still in full swing; there was some guy onstage laughing and posing to the strains of "I'm Too Sexy." Marianne made her way through the crowd to the bar.

"Warren!" she called. Her cousin handed a couple of luridly colored cocktails to a customer and then turned to her.

"Marianne!" he cried. "Hot damn woman, you rule!"

He leaned over the bar and hugged her.

"I need to borrow twenty-four dollars," Marianne told him. "And I need the rest of the night off."

"After that performance, hon, you can have whatever you want." He pulled his wallet from his pocket and handed her the money. "Does this mean you're doing your date tonight?"

Marianne smiled broadly. "Cuz, tonight I'm doing whatever the heck I want."

"In that case, you should take these." Warren reached underneath the bar near the cash register and held up a small box.

Condoms.

The sight of the little box suddenly made this all much more real to her. She was going off with a complete stranger. With condoms. And she didn't even know his last name.

For a moment she hesitated.

Warren's eyes narrowed. "Marianne? Are you—do you know who Oz is, really?"

No. And that was the problem.

Everything in her upbringing, everything she'd done for her entire life, protested at the idea of running off with a man she'd barely met with no more protection than a pack of condoms.

She didn't know Oz. And yet she did. Marianne remembered being swept up into his arms, kissed as if she were precious. How he'd told her to put on more protective clothing. How, when she'd been with him, she'd said exactly what she'd wanted to.

He was dangerous and yet somehow, with him, she was safe.

"I know how he makes me feel," she said, and took the box of condoms.

"That's my girl." Warren grinned. "Y'all stay out as long as you want, now. Just—" he grabbed her elbow as she was turning away, and his voice was serious again "—be careful, okay? You've only been here since yesterday. And while I'm all for having fun on the rebound, it isn't long since you kissed Mr. Perfect goodbye."

"I'll be careful," Marianne promised him. "It's for fun, Warren, and I need some fun. I'm not going to fall in love with the guy."

Marianne went to the table at the side of the room where two of the women from the charity were collecting bids. They greeted her with wide smiles and handshakes.

"You got a wicked good-lookin' man there," one of them said as Marianne counted out the cash for them.

"'Wicked' is right," she said. "I love bad boys."

The two women exchanged looks. "You're not from around here, are you?"

"No, but I think I'm gonna like it," she answered. She stuck the receipt in her back pocket next to the condoms, and headed toward the entrance.

The front door of the bar was glass. Marianne paused before she opened it and saw, on the road outside the bar, Oz standing by his motorcycle. Somehow in the few minutes away from him she'd forgotten how sexy he was. How the mere sight of him made her feel as if she'd been kicked in the stomach.

If it were possible to be kicked in the stomach and keep wanting to come back for more.

The streetlights lit his blond hair and gilded his shoulders. His bare arms were crossed over his chest. He was looking at his bike as if he were studying it, and he looked calm, thoughtful. While Marianne's heart was palpitating like a horny bullfrog on a summer night.

She watched her breath mist on the glass and realized she was hesitating before opening the door.

She blinked and swallowed hard. She wanted this. She wanted this a lot.

It was all about this man, this bike, and this night.

Marianne pushed open the door.

He didn't wait for her to come to him; he met her halfway across the sidewalk and stood close, but not touching. "I was beginning to think I'd dreamed you," he said.

"It took me a few minutes to find the three thousand dollars."

"Nobody's ever paid three thousand dollars for the pleasure of my company before," Oz said, and then appeared to reconsider his words. "Not up front, anyway."

"I'm betting you're worth it," Marianne replied, and she wondered how these flirtatious words came so easily when she was with Oz.

"I'll do my best." He looked her up and down and Marianne couldn't resist a shiver. "The sneakers are okay, but you'll be cold on the back of the bike with just a sweater. Here."

He held out his black leather jacket to her. Marianne took it and slipped it on.

The jacket hung halfway down her thighs and several inches past her fingertips. It felt as if his arms were around her again. She ducked her head inside the collar and smelled Oz: leather, spice, soap, man.

"Won't you get cold?" she asked.

He was still looking at her. "I don't think so."

The meaning behind his words gave her another kick in the stomach.

"Are you ready to go?" she asked.

"Yeah." But he didn't move toward the bike. Instead he reached forward and zipped up the jacket. His hand brushed her chin when it got to the top of the zipper, and he kept it there. She felt as if the gentle pressure of his knuckle on her skin were the only thing keeping her upright.

"I wish I had a helmet for you," he said.

She couldn't help laughing at this badass man worrying about safety gear. "Do you have one for yourself?"

He shook his head. "The law doesn't require it. But risking someone else's life is different."

There was a crease between his eyebrows. Marianne

reached up and touched it with her finger. Her hand on his face, his on hers.

"I'll trust you not to crash," she said.

He nodded. "That'll have to do. Let's go." He took her hand and led her to the Harley. His skin was warm and she could feel calluses on his palms and his fingers.

From riding the motorcycle, she thought. She wondered what his rough hands would feel like against her soft belly. Her skin tightened and loosened at the same time.

He straddled the bike and held it steady for her as she climbed on behind him. "Ever ridden one of these before?" he asked her over his shoulder.

"Never."

"Low riders are built for comfort rather than speed, but this one will go pretty fast anyway. You should hold on tight to me."

As if she needed to be asked twice. Marianne scooted forward on the leather seat so her thighs were close against Oz's legs. She wrapped her arms around his waist and leaned forward against his back.

He felt wonderful. His back was strong and broad; she could feel him breathing. She rested her head on his black cotton T-shirt between his shoulder blades and she could hear his heartbeat, every breath he took. And his smell—the same smell as his jacket, clean and masculine.

Her hands rested on the firm muscles of his stomach. She tightened her fingers on him, breathing in Oz and the hot chrome and oil of the Harley.

In the parking lot, after he'd kissed her, he'd had a hard-on. She'd seen its length beneath his faded jeans and it had sent a thrill through her. She wondered if he was still aroused.

If she let her hands creep just a few inches lower, she'd know.

Marianne was definitely aroused. With her legs open to straddle the motorcycle and Oz, the seam of her jeans pressed against her crotch and made her feel tender and swollen. Wearing jeans had seemed like a good idea, but now they were too tight. She shifted on the seat, resisting the urge to push even closer and rub herself against him.

Good grief. Now she was thinking about behaving like a dog in heat.

"Try to keep yourself still," Oz said, and she felt and heard his voice through his body, low and vibrating. "Lean into me and follow my lead. We have to let our bodies work together with the bike."

His muscles underneath her cheek and arms and hands were hard. He felt tense. She saw and felt him shake his head slightly, and take a deep breath. Her breasts flattened against him.

"Relax," he said. She wasn't sure if he was speaking to her or to himself, but she loosened her grip a little. More like embracing him than clinging on for dear life.

He started the engine and Marianne gasped. The bike rumbled underneath her and suddenly her whole body was vibrating with it. She'd been too overwhelmed on the stage to appreciate the feeling of sitting behind a strong man on a powerful machine.

But she did now.

Her legs trembled. The fabric of her T-shirt thrummed against her nipples. Her body moved against Oz like a million tiny caresses. And between her legs there was an irresistible warm throb, like a teasing, insistent hand.

Or mouth.

It was the most exquisite foreplay she'd ever experienced, and they hadn't even moved yet. They were still at the curb in front of the bar, the noise of the Harley's engine filling the empty street.

"Oz?" She stretched up so she could speak close to his ear. "What are you waiting for?"

"I'm trying to remind myself to concentrate on the road and not you wrapped around me." He spoke quietly, but she could hear him even above the engine.

"Oh," she said. So he was turned on too. The knowledge was even better foreplay than the motorcycle.

"Do—do you think you can concentrate on the road?" she asked shakily.

"I'll try. Hold on."

The Harley roared and they leapt forward. The air rushed around her and she was pulled backward by the jerk of speed. Marianne cried out and tightened her arms and legs around Oz.

Marianne Webb was on a big, bad motorcycle with the hunkiest man she'd ever seen. She grinned against Oz's T-shirt.

And then shrieked as the motorcycle engine suddenly cut out, throwing her forward against Oz. Her forehead and nose banged hard on his shoulder blade; her breasts flattened against his back.

In an instant he'd turned half around. "Are you all right?"

She rubbed her nose. "I'm fine. What happened?"

Oz's face was sheepish. "I slipped the clutch and stalled it. Sorry."

She couldn't help giggling. He looked like a very tall,

strong little boy who'd been caught doing something wrong. "Mind not on the road?"

"No. I haven't ridden—I mean I haven't had a passenger for a long time."

When he shifted his weight back so he was facing forward, his denim-clad backside brushed against her groin, and she nearly groaned as pleasure shot up through her body.

Then the Harley started up again and she did groan at the vibrations on her oversensitized nerve endings. Nipples, inner thighs, clitoris.

Was it possible to have an orgasm just from riding on a motorcycle? she wondered. And then they were moving again and she stopped wondering about anything.

It was just so…incredible.

They reached the end of the road and she felt the bike tipping over. Oz was leaning, they both were leaning, and—they were going to fall.

She gasped, her eyes wide, her stomach about to leap through her throat.

They turned left. Miraculously, didn't fall. Kept going.

Then a right turn, the two of them on the bike leaning together. Their bodies and the bike working as one, as Oz had said.

"Wow," she said to the air rushing by her face.

And then they were on a long straight stretch of road and Oz gunned the engine and they sped up. Not much, probably—they were in a business area—but enough so that she felt the wind in her hair. The speed was so much more immediate than in a car. Her feet, propped up on the bike, were inches from the road as it rushed beneath them. When she looked away from Oz's back she had a clear view of the buildings they passed, lit up by streetlights and signs and the lights inside. Even the shadows seemed clearer than they would through a car window.

And the smells. She could smell the leaves on the trees. The autumn air. The tarry smell of warm roads cooling at night. The drunken smell of gasoline.

"This is great!" she yelled at the back of Oz's blond head, hearing her words whipping away behind her, and she felt him laughing.

"Wait until I get us onto the highway," Oz said. His words came back to her with the wind. They turned left again, onto a bridge, and Marianne could smell the salty, slightly rank odor of the sea and feel the freshness of the air against her face.

And then, open road. Four lanes, two of them theirs.

Oz gunned the motor and they shot forward. The speed turned Marianne's guts to liquid. The trees by the side of the road blurred into dark shadows and the scent of pine. She sucked in a breath of pure exhilaration. "Yeeeee-haw!" she yelled to the wind and the stars above them, the only things standing still in a world of movement and joy. She threw back her head, felt her hair flying free of her ponytail.

She had no idea how fast they were going—she only knew it was faster than she'd ever gone before. It was like soaring through the air, though she could feel the road beneath her and the power of the bike. So much force and energy.

All of it controlled by Oz.

Who was between her thighs.

She laughed.

Two days ago she had left her old life swearing to

become somebody new. And so far, she was doing a marvelous job.

She was free, she was herself and she could do anything she wanted to in the world.

"Can you hear me?" she shouted to Oz through the wind and the motor and the speed.

The wind was flicking his hair around like a chaotic halo. He moved his head a little to the side, obviously sensing that she'd said something.

"I can't hear you," he said. Of course his voice carried behind him, but hers couldn't reach forward.

"I want to have wild torrid sex with you!" she yelled.

"What?"

"Nothing!" She tossed her head back again and shook the last of her hair free. The elastic band fell off, lost to the road. She pushed herself up so her mouth was right by his ear.

"Faster!" she shouted, and Oz nodded.

She dug her fingers into the muscles of his stomach and tightened her legs around his hips, and everything became pure adrenaline.

It seemed like delicious hours before Oz slowed, and pulled the bike up by the side of the road. Marianne couldn't see anything there but shrubs and trees.

He cut the engine. Marianne's ears rang.

"I want to show you something," he said. His normal speaking voice was loud in the echo left by the Harley's motor.

He put down the kickstand and got off the bike, holding out his hand for her. Her legs trembled when she stepped onto the ground. The road felt as if it were shaking.

She stumbled a step toward him and clutched on to his arm to steady herself.

"Gosh, I can tell why you ride one of these things," she said. "It's sex on wheels, isn't it?"

"More than usual, this time," he said. "Are you all right?"

"I'm practically delirious."

He smiled. "I know how you feel."

Her legs felt more used to the ground, now. She raised a hand to push her hair out of her face and her fingers stuck in the tangles.

"Stay here for a minute," Oz said. "I need to check something. I'll be right back."

He gave her hand a squeeze before turning and disappearing into the bushes at the side of the road.

What was he doing? she wondered, trying to finger-comb the snarls out of her hair. Taking a leak? Finding some secret biker hangout? She heard the bushes rustle for a moment, and then it was quiet.

Very quiet. It must be late. A breeze whispered through some drying autumn leaves. The Harley's engine ticked as it cooled. She could hear the muffled surge of the ocean; they were still on the coast. The houses across the street were dark.

Probably past midnight, she thought. Her breath formed little clouds in the moonlight.

Marianne shivered and abandoned her attempt to fix her hair. She shoved her hands into the pockets of Oz's jacket.

Her fingers encountered something in one of the pockets. It felt like a leather wallet, but there was something else too. She pulled them out.

A black leather wallet, and a small cellophane-wrapped package which felt familiar.

There was a Post-it note stuck to the top of the package.

Oz—Remember I get a beer for every one you use. Jack.

She peeled off the note. It was a box of condoms. Identical to the one that was in the back pocket of her jeans right now.

She replaced the note and put the box and the wallet back in Oz's pocket.

Was this some sort of sign?

Or maybe a warning?

The bushes parted and a big, dark shape stepped out. It was completely in shadow and Marianne almost knew it was Oz, but she stepped backward and groped for the motorcycle anyway.

What are you doing out here in the middle of the night in the middle of nowhere with a man you don't know and no keys for the motorcycle and no idea how to drive it? her brain asked her, and she felt sweat breaking out on the palms of her hands and her heart jumping into her throat.

"It's me," Oz said. He was so tall. She couldn't see his face but she saw the shadows of his broad shoulders, his big hands.

She stopped, the backs of her legs touching the motorcycle. Her heart didn't slow down, though.

What on earth was she doing?

It wasn't just that she didn't know Oz. She didn't know any people like Oz, either. She'd never been in a situation like this.

She should go back to Warren's and concentrate on

learning how to make a margarita. Her new life could come one step at a time. She didn't need to jump right in with both feet and both boxes of condoms.

"Oz—" she started, and then Oz stepped forward and the moonlight caught his hair and his face. His straight nose, full lips. The smile grooves on either side of his mouth. His eyes glimmered in the silver moonlight.

He was so perfect she could hardly see straight, and she didn't want to go home anymore.

"Is Oz your real name?" she asked.

"It's a nickname."

"How'd you get it? From Ozzy Osbourne?" Bikers listened to heavy metal music, right?

He chuckled. "No. From my youngest sister, Daisy. My real name's Oscar. She couldn't pronounce it when she was little so she called me Oz. It stuck."

She nodded, feeling silly. She'd met the dangerous motorcycle hoodlum at a charity auction and he had been given his nickname by a little kid called Daisy.

Odds were, he wasn't a crazed psycho killer.

"I didn't think you looked much like Ozzy," she said.

"I've never bitten the head off a bat or peed on the Alamo, either."

He stepped closer to her. "I loved having you holding on to me on the bike, but I think I like you better like this. I can see how beautiful you are."

He smoothed her tangled hair back with one of his big, gentle hands, and shook his head slightly. "I didn't expect to meet someone like you tonight."

Marianne had to remind herself to breathe.

She might not know Oz. But as she'd said to Warren, she knew how he made her feel: reckless and beautiful and full of desire.

Like the person she wanted to be.

She took his hand in hers and kissed it. His warm skin smelled just slightly of engine oil.

"What do you want to show me?" she asked.

CHAPTER FOUR

"THROUGH here."

The bushes blocked out most of the moonlight, but Marianne could make out the deeper shadow of Oz just ahead of her. She stepped forward and saw that he was holding aside a branch.

"There's a hole in the fence," he said. "It's a squeeze for me, but I think you'll make it through easy."

She couldn't see the fence clearly but she could see the moonlight on the other side of the hole. "What's in there?" she asked.

"Go ahead. You'll see."

Trespassing. That was illegal.

Good. Beyond a parking ticket or two, Marianne had never broken any laws before. She wasn't even a litterbug.

She slipped through the fence and through another less dense bush, and found herself on a wide, mowed lawn. She couldn't see a house anywhere. A path gleamed white to her left.

She knew Oz had come through and was standing behind her because she could feel him. "Where are we?" she whispered.

"Just south of Portland. Come on." He took her by the hand again and strode toward the path.

"I used to sneak in through that hole when I was a teenager," Oz said as they walked. She noticed he was talking aloud, apparently unafraid of being caught. "I'm amazed it hasn't been fixed."

"Why'd you sneak in here?" Now that she could look around, it looked like some sort of park. Grass stretched out all around her.

"To be alone. I had five younger brothers and sisters at home. Sometimes I just wanted quiet." He stopped walking, and she stopped with him. "Listen. You can't even tell we're within a couple miles of a city."

A dog barked in the distance. They listened to the quiet for a moment, and then started walking again. The air was fresher on her face and she could smell the ocean now, too.

"You have five brothers and sisters?" Marianne asked.

"I was an only child for four years before Michael came along. Then Jennifer, the twins Alice and Joe, and then Daisy. They made a lot of noise."

"Your mother must've been a busy woman."

"She was extremely busy."

His tone had changed, almost imperceptibly, with that statement. From good humor to something else. She looked over at him, but couldn't quite make out his expression in the moonlight.

"What was it like to be part of such a big family?"

"Well, I learned a lot about sibling rivalry." His voice was light again.

"It must have been nice not to be your parents' only hope," Marianne said, and then snapped her mouth shut.

Why'd she say that? She certainly did not need to

discuss the pressure she'd felt under at home with this guy she'd just met. Or how she'd failed.

Especially when she'd left it all behind her for good.

"I mean, I bet it was fun sometimes, even if it was noisy," she said.

"My brothers and sisters are the best. I was the eldest, so I had a lot of responsibility for them. But at least I didn't have to wear any of the hand-me-downs." Oz's eyes met hers as they walked. "You're an only child?"

"Yes."

"That can be lonely."

She laughed. "I was spoiled rotten, just how I like it." She winked at him again. "I'm the type of girl who demands instant gratification. In everything."

"That doesn't surprise me." But he was still looking at her and she could tell that something was going on in his brain.

For the first time she noticed consciously that his face was intelligent as well as beautiful.

And what was wrong with that? There was no law that said a rebel couldn't be smart. Look at her: she was smart, and she was rebelling against every image that anyone had ever had of her, just by being here.

Still, something about his eyes searching her face unnerved her. As if he could see right inside her, every fault and every fear.

She tore her eyes away from his, and then saw where they were, and stopped.

"Oh," she said.

They were standing just above a small sandy ocean cove on a bank of boulders. The waves, frosted with moonlight, frothed over the sand and licked the rocks below them. To their right, a silver-shining tower rose from the black coastline. As she watched a white light blinked on from the top of the tower and then blinked off again.

"It's the Portland Head Light. Oldest lighthouse in Maine." Oz sat down on the ground and patted the grass beside him. She sat, too.

"It's beautiful," she said.

"You should hear it when there's fog. It sounds like a powerful ghost."

Oz put his arm around her and pulled her closer to his side. He felt very solid and very strong and very warm. From this angle, sitting close to him, she could see how finely drawn his features were, the preciseness of his nose and the keenness of his eyes. The fullness of his lips.

Marianne looked back at the lighthouse. It blinked white light again, like a close star.

"'A pillar of fire by night,'" Oz said. "That's what Longfellow called it."

"Cold fire, maybe," she said. "Beautiful, perfect, and alone."

Marianne shivered at the pain that pierced her gut with those words.

Oz tightened his arm around her shoulders. "Are you all right, Marianne?"

She breathed in and smelled and tasted the sea air and Oz.

She wasn't alone tonight. And she wasn't like that perfect, lonely lighthouse anymore. She'd moved up here to change: to become happy and carefree.

And reckless.

"Stop talking and kiss me," she said.

She twisted in his embrace, took his head in her

hands, and pulled him toward her. His mouth met hers and she heard that rumble in his throat again.

Their first kiss, on the stage in front of all those people, had been gentle. Almost chaste, except for that deep, hungry sound Oz had made.

This kiss wasn't anything like chaste.

His lips were cool from the night air but they parted on hers right away and his mouth was hot. With the first touch, Marianne tightened her grip on his head, tangling her fingers in his wild hair and pulling him still closer.

They kissed in bites, as if they were devouring each other. Her tongue met his. He tasted of toothpaste and sweet, sexy man.

His tongue was inside her, his breath on her lips in sharp gasps. Marianne sucked his full lower lip into her mouth, tested it between her teeth like something delicious.

Oz groaned again and kissed her still harder. He was strong and hot and wild and everything she'd wanted him to be, and Marianne felt the desire that had been simmering inside her boil over. It swept through her entire body to pool heat between her legs, in her mouth, in her belly, everywhere.

She'd never been kissed like this before. She wasn't sure if any of the other kisses she'd ever had really counted as kisses, next to this one.

He grabbed her hips and pulled her onto his lap, not letting their lips part. She moved so she faced him and her legs were wrapped around his body. Unlike on the bike, she rested on his lap, feeling his hard legs beneath her and his hard chest against her.

Savage wanting. No finesse, no style, just—hunger.

She felt his hands fumbling with the zipper of his

jacket she was wearing, kissing her all the time as he pushed it off her shoulders. And then his hands were on her bare arms, running over her naked flesh beneath his hands. The sounds their mouths made as they kissed were wet and frankly sexual. His mouth demanding, his tongue thrusting into her. She heard herself moaning.

Oz took her head in his big hands and pulled his mouth back. She opened her eyes to look into his. They were wide and gleaming in the moonlight.

Their breath came in harsh pants, louder than the ocean, kissing each other's faces.

"Marianne." Oz's voice was rough. "You're incredible."

She didn't want to talk; she wanted to feel. Marianne pressed her mouth against his jaw, where the skin was clean-shaven but just a little bit rough. She tasted him, clean and a little salty, like the smell of the ocean.

When she kissed his neck she could feel his pulse hammering.

"Marianne," he said again, and it sounded half like pleasure, half like a plea.

She wanted her hands to touch him like her mouth. Marianne took her fingers out of his silky hair and put them on his broad, bare shoulders. Her palms curled around his muscles. She remembered him controlling the Harley, and shuddered.

The moonlight made everything black, gray and silver, but she knew the skin of his arms was golden. She slid her hands down the length of his upper arms, slowly, feeling every bulge of muscle and sinew. The skin on his right arm felt different, somehow—cooler, slightly slicker.

That's where his tattoo is, she thought. She'd never felt a tattoo before. Maybe it was scar tissue that made the skin feel different.

She ran her hands back up his arms to check they were as perfect as they'd felt the first time. They were. He pressed a wild kiss onto her forehead, and on each of her eyebrows.

"You're driving me crazy," he breathed.

Marianne knew that the smile on her lips was devilish.

"You didn't bring me here to talk, did you?" she asked in a low voice.

He blinked, and then he smiled, digging those lines in his cheeks.

"I do like talking with you," he said. "But I have to admit that when I brought you to the biggest phallic symbol in the neighborhood I hoped you'd have other ideas."

He nudged her hips forward, right up against him, and she felt his erection pressing between her legs. Hot and hard through two layers of denim.

"That is a pretty blatant phallic symbol," Marianne said. "The lighthouse isn't bad either."

How was she thinking up this stuff?

Who cared?

She arched against Oz. Her breasts pressed into his chest, sending pleasure so sharp it was almost pain through her body. And her over-aroused crotch rubbed against the length of his penis.

She caught her breath. Oz let out his in a gasp.

"I think I mentioned Longfellow, too," he said.

With his hands around her waist he slid her up against him again. Root to tip, and back down.

It was her turn to gasp.

"Longfellow? You're pretty sure of yourself, aren't you?" she managed.

"I'm definitely feeling like a pillar of fire," he said, and captured her mouth with his.

This kiss was slower, less carnal, more sensuous, and Marianne felt herself melting. His hands guided her up and down on him again, and again. He growled low in his throat and the vibrations from it traveled from her lips down her throat, through her body.

Just as she'd thought, his hands nearly reached right around her waist. He slid them down her hips, and then around to cup her bottom. He felt so…big. Everywhere.

This man has spent what feels like hours between my legs already and I haven't even taken off his chaps yet, she thought dazedly.

How good was this going to be once they were actually naked?

She groaned as her mind filled with a picture of them just like this, her on Oz's lap, him moving her up and down on him. But both of them naked. Her breasts brushing against the blond hair on his chest, his perfect bare arms around her.

And that glorious hardness inside her.

She felt herself break out in a sweat, and heard herself groan.

Oz stopped the kiss, breathing hard. "What's this?" He felt her backside.

"Honey, if you don't know what that is, I'm not sure I should be here."

He laughed, a short sudden burst that forced him up between her legs even harder. They both gasped.

"I meant what's this?" He slipped his long fingers

into the pocket of her jeans, and brought out a little box and a slip of paper.

The condoms Warren had given her, and the receipt for her three-thousand-dollar date.

Marianne watched him examine what he held. It took a moment for him to read the package in the dim light.

He raised his eyebrows and licked his lips, looking like a grown-up little boy who'd just seen a whole jar of candy he couldn't quite believe was his.

"Um," he said. "Are these something you carry around with you all the time? Or did you bring them specifically for this date?"

"For this date," she admitted.

In an instant she was on her back on the ground, and Oz was over her. The grass was cool and a little damp. It was a delicious contrast to Oz's body, hot and so, so good pressed against the length of her, his leather-clad thigh in between her legs.

He kissed her, another carnal, seductive kiss.

Then he propped himself up on one arm and put his other hand to her cheek and pinched it softly. He ran his fingertips over her face, tracing her features, his eyes watching his hand. It wasn't a sexual touch. Instead it was intense, intimate in a way that went beyond just desire.

"What are you doing, Oz?" she whispered.

"I'm making sure you're real," he said. "Not one of my fantasies." He stroked along her jawline, and down to her neck.

"Do you usually have problems telling fantasy apart from reality?"

This gentle touch was turning her on even more, if

possible, than the blatantly sexual thrusting and groping they'd been doing two minutes ago.

"No. I'm usually pretty attuned to reality. But tonight's been different." He tilted his head to watch his fingers go down her neck. They met the first button of her blouse and he undid it. Oz dipped his head to the V opening he'd made and she felt him inhale her, and then brush his lips over her collarbone.

"I couldn't have imagined anything as pure as your skin," he murmured. He unfastened another button. Another. And kissed her between her breasts. His hair tickled her neck, and his fingers feathered over the lace trimming of one cup of her bra.

Marianne abruptly became aware of a sensation she'd never had before. Her breasts were demanding to be touched. More than demanding. They were screaming to be touched. As if Oz didn't touch her breasts right, right now, her breasts were going to drive her insane.

She'd liked having her breasts touched, before. But she'd never needed to have them touched. Never craved it.

Marianne held her breath.

And then Oz slipped his fingers underneath the lace of her bra, molded his big hand around her, ran the pad of his thumb over her nipple, kissed the side of her other breast still inside its cup, and Marianne let out a sound that was nearly a scream.

She heard Oz whisper, "Beautiful," before he pushed her bra down, freed her nipple to the cool night air and immediately replaced it with his hot mouth.

The pleasure was so great she didn't know what to do. Instinctively she arched upward, twining her left leg around his, bucking her hips against him.

At first his lips sucked her, then she felt his tongue and teeth rasp over her. She tightened her legs around him. Sweet friction between her legs, caused by her jeans and his hips; the magic worked by his hand and his mouth on her skin.

It was building fast, growing in her belly like a hunger. Marianne dug her fingers of one hand into Oz's shoulder. The other reached downward to the leg that pressed against her, grabbing the warm, smooth leather of his chaps. Trying to bring him nearer to her, at the same time that she reached for satisfaction.

Oz lifted his head from her skin. The cold air on her nipple felt like part of his caress, and Marianne groaned.

"Marianne," he said, and she tried to focus on his face, through the haze of pleasure. His beautiful, sexy face, half lit by the moon.

"Tell me what you want," he said. "Because in a minute I'm going to lose control here." She saw him swallow, saw the muscles in his jaw clench. "Tell me you want this as much as I want you."

His words, *I want you,* sent another throb through her body. So close. She was poised on the edge of release. Another shifting of his body, another touch of Oz's mouth on her nipple or her neck, and she was going to throw herself into wild abandonment. Take him, glut herself with pleasure.

She wanted him. She was hungry for him. More than she'd been hungry for anything, since—

Marianne gasped, and stiffened in Oz's embrace.

The last time she'd wanted anything this badly, she'd nearly killed herself for it.

The realization froze her to the spot, turned her hands on Oz's body into clumsy mittens.

Oz stilled on her. "Marianne? What's wrong?"

She opened her mouth but no words came out.

I can't. I can't want this much. I'm not supposed to.

Oz lifted himself off and away from her. He lay beside her on the grass and put a gentle hand on her shoulder. "Hey. It's okay. Are you all right?"

Without him, she was cold. She sat up and fastened her blouse with shaking fingers.

Her body wanted Oz back. Her body hurt and hungered and demanded the orgasm he'd been about to give her.

She was good at ignoring what her body wanted. She'd spent nearly a year hardly eating anything, after all. Getting thinner and thinner until she was almost gone.

Marianne tried to push back her hair, but her fingers got stuck in the tangles. She glanced down at herself: her blouse was wrinkled all to heck. Her mouth felt swollen, tender.

She stood up. Oz stood up next to her. Their breath was coming fast and it made clouds in the air.

"Marianne," he said. "Can you tell me what's wrong?" He didn't touch her this time, but she felt him anyway.

Could she tell him what was wrong? *Sorry, Oz, having sex with you reminds me of the time I just about killed myself.* She didn't think so.

"I just want to go home, okay?" Her voice sounded strange to her.

Oz stood next to her and looked at her with his keen eyes, and she could tell he was thinking again, trying to see inside her. She turned away and began to brush the damp grass off her jeans.

He picked up his jacket off the ground and put it back over her shoulders. "Okay, let's go," he said.

She nodded. As she picked a last blade of grass off

the top of her sneaker she saw the glimmer of white paper by her shoe. She stooped and picked up her receipt and her box of condoms, feeling herself blush.

Some reckless woman she was. She'd done a lousy job of changing her life. She couldn't even manage to use a single condom.

She shoved them back into her jeans pocket and then put her arms through Oz's jacket.

As they turned to walk back to the broken fence, she heard the lighthouse's fog signal for the first time.

As Oz had said, it sounded like a powerful ghost.

Marianne gritted her teeth and leaned her head against Oz's back. The last Harley ride had been exhilarating, but this one was torture.

Oz between her legs again, but this time she had the memory of his hands on her, his mouth, his body on top of hers. The Harley's vibrations massaged every single erogenous zone she had. Maddening. Reminding her of her failure.

What sort of bad girl chickened out at the last minute? Right when she was about to have incredible sex with a physically perfect man in a beautiful place?

She tried breathing in the night air, but she only smelled Oz. She closed her eyes and felt her hair whipping around her face. She was probably never going to be able to comb out the snarls.

What kind of bad girl worried about combing her hair?

She felt sick with frustrated desire and self-blame. She closed her eyes, clenched her fists, pressed her head against Oz's back and endured the rest of the ride.

They slowed, pulled up to the curb, and Oz cut out the engine. She let go of him and climbed off the motorcycle onto the sidewalk in front of the bar. It was closed and dark.

"Where do you live?" Oz asked, getting off the motorcycle himself.

"Up above the bar. I'm okay from here. Thank you."

"It's late and it's dark. I'll walk you to your door."

The motorcycle rebel is a gentleman, she thought, leading Oz down the alley by the side of the bar and round to the parking lot in the back. He'd been right; the alley and parking lot were full of shadows. And she was glad for his strong, safe presence.

She snorted under her breath. Pathetic.

The door to the stairs up to her apartment was beside the bar fire exit. She stopped. "Well, goodnight," she said, beginning to pull off Oz's jacket.

"I'll see you safe inside," he said.

She shrugged his jacket back on, and dug out her key. The door led to a dark, steep, narrow staircase.

"Go on up," Oz said behind her. "I'll come with you."

Even though she couldn't see Oz, she could feel and hear and smell him as he followed her up the stairs. At the top, she found the light switch and flipped it on.

She had to blink at its brightness. The walls were stained dingy yellow, the floor was scuffed, and a long dusty cobweb dangled from the lightbulb. And Oz was tall, wild-haired, golden-skinned, even more beautiful than he'd been in the moonlight.

Stupid, stupid Goody Two-shoes.

She turned away from him and unlocked her door.

"Marianne," Oz said, "let's not leave it like this. Can I take you out tomorrow night? On a real date?"

"I'm working in the bar."

"Tomorrow afternoon, then. I'll take you out to lunch. We can talk."

"Sounds wild," she said dully. "Lunch and talking."

"Please, Marianne. I want to know who you are."

Who she was. As if somebody like him, someone free and rebellious, was going to want to know somebody uptight and straight like her.

She took off his jacket. It was big and heavy and warm and felt like a part of him. She didn't want to give it up.

Marianne shook her head and shoved his jacket back at him, more violently than she'd intended. As he caught it something fell out of the pocket and hit the wooden floor with a dull thump and a skitter.

Oz's wallet. Marianne stooped to pick it up, glad to have an excuse not to look at him anymore. It had landed upside down, and a credit card had come out and slid a little way across the floor.

Gold card. A motorcycle rebel with a good credit rating.

She picked it up. It gleamed in the harsh light. The name across the bottom said **DR. OSCAR STRUMMER.**

Marianne's eyes widened. Her heart thumped.

She stood up and held out the card to Oz. Leather-clad, tattooed Oz, wearing boots with chains and a Harley Davidson T-shirt with its arms torn off.

"You're a *doctor?*"

CHAPTER FIVE

"UM," OZ said. "Yes."

"A real doctor? Like, a fine upstanding member of the community?"

He at least had the good sense to look a little sheepish. "I'm not a physician. I've got a Ph.D. But an upstanding member of the community, yes."

"Why on earth are you dressed up like a motorcycle rebel?"

Oz looked down at himself. He tugged on one of his chaps. "I thought you liked it," he said.

Marianne's mouth dropped open. "I—" Her eyes fell on the tattoo on his right arm. In the bright light thrown by the naked lightbulb, she could see that the bottom of it was peeling off.

She remembered how it had felt slipperier than skin. She'd thought that was what tattoos felt like.

"That tattoo's fake, isn't it?" she asked.

He glanced at it. "Fortunately. Snakes and swords aren't really my thing."

"What—?" Marianne clenched her fists, replaying the evening in her head in the light of the new knowledge that she'd been trying to discover her wicked side with a man who had a gold card and a Ph.D.

"What kind of a person are you?" she said. "You lied to me!"

"I didn't—"

She felt her face going red and her heart hammering. "Is this some kind of kinky thing for you, to dress up like somebody you aren't and then get strangers to have sex with you?"

Oz took a step back on the landing and held up his hands. "Hey, wait a minute, I didn't set out to seduce you."

"You had condoms in your pocket and you were expecting to use them!"

He looked taken aback. "I had condoms in my pocket?"

She pointed at his jacket. He rummaged in the pocket and pulled out the box of condoms and the Post-it note.

"Oh," he said, reading. "These are from my friend Jack."

"It says he gets a beer for every one you use. What do y'all have, some sort of bet going about whether you'd get lucky?"

Oz shook his head. "It's not a bet, it's a long-standing arrangement. When Jack met the woman he was going to marry, he—"

"Bet you a beer that he'd screw her?" Marianne was way past caring about her language.

Oz's mouth fell open. "I—"

"I don't believe I was so stupid."

She stormed into her apartment and flung the door shut behind her.

Oz caught it before it slammed.

"Marianne," he said, standing in the doorway. "Calm down and think about this. I tried to tell you who I was, but you asked me not to. And you had a package of condoms in your pocket, too. I can see you're angry. But it's not me you're angry at."

She wheeled around to face him. "Who am I angry at then?"

He stepped into the room, cautiously, his eyes on hers. "I'd guess that you're angry at yourself," he said.

It was her turn to stand open-mouthed.

Oz was right. He hadn't done anything that she hadn't asked him to do. And she had asked him not to tell her who he really was. He was a gentleman in chaps and studded boots. If she'd judged from impressions, that was her own fault, not his.

And she was spitting mad at herself. Because she hadn't been able to start her new life when she'd had the chance.

"What the heck are you, some kind of amateur psychologist or something?"

"No, a professional one." Oz looked around for a chair. The only one had a pile of neatly folded clothes on it. Instead, he leaned against the wall next to the door. She could tell the stance was meant to lessen the impact of his physical presence, make himself seem smaller, less imposing. It didn't really work.

"I'm a clinical psychologist," he said. "I've got my own therapeutic practice and I lecture at the university."

Marianne closed her eyes and buried her face in her hands. "Oh, cripes. You're exactly the kind of man my parents would want me to date."

"Is that a bad thing?" he asked gently.

After Jason? Yes.

When she wanted to become a whole new person? Definitely.

She dropped her hands and took a deep breath. "Why did you dress up like that?"

Oz looked down at what he was wearing again. "My friends thought it would help me raise more money for the youth center."

She laughed without humor. "Well, that worked."

"It wasn't supposed to mislead anybody. I thought most of the bidders would be local."

Meaning that she was the only one who'd been fooled by his getup. Marianne remembered the look the two women had exchanged when she'd said how much she liked bad boys. They'd known who Oz really was.

She felt like five hundred kinds of an idiot.

"Is the Harley yours, at least?"

He shook his head.

Marianne sighed.

"Oz—Dr. Strummer—I'd really like you to leave now."

Oz stepped toward her. "Marianne, this doesn't have to be a problem."

His eyes were intelligent and perceptive. They could look right inside her.

A clinical psychologist, for goodness sake. Exactly what she did not need.

"Thank you for your time, Dr. Strummer." She fell back into her Southern debutante voice: sweet, polite, and brooking no disagreement. A steel magnolia. "Goodnight."

He looked as if he wanted to say something else. Then he looked as if he thought better of it.

"Goodnight," he said, and left, closing the door

gently after him. She heard his heavy boots going down her rickety stairs.

Marianne threw herself onto her bed and covered her head with the pillow.

Oz gunned the motor and cruised down the empty road away from the bar and Marianne.

He'd been studying human nature for almost as long as he could remember, starting from learning child psychology from all of his younger brothers and sisters while he'd been looking after them. And he still couldn't figure out what the hell had just happened.

Moonlight, the lighthouse, the most attractive woman he'd ever met in his arms. It had been a fantasy come to life. Perfect—and with every touch, every taste, it had been getting more perfect.

And then his perfect woman had…freaked out. That wasn't the clinical term for it, but it fit.

The woman obviously had some issues. From the way she'd avoided talking about her past, they were most likely rooted there. And she didn't have any apparent interest in working them out.

Not the kind of thing you need, Oz, he told himself, steering the bike around a corner. *You need an escape from your career, not another person to help cure.*

He sighed. It was probably better the reality came out now, before he'd become emotionally involved.

This late at night—or early in the morning—the streets were deserted. Oz nudged the bike a little faster, just over the speed limit, so he could feel the cool air against his face.

He remembered her arms around his waist. The taste of her skin on his lips. Her gasps of pleasure.

How she'd yelled, "I want to have wild torrid sex with you!" when she'd thought he couldn't hear her.

Oz smiled. Marianne had paid three thousand dollars for him, kissed him in front of an audience, and then yelled that. If he'd wanted an escape from his daily life, he couldn't have done much better.

He turned into Jack and Kitty's neighborhood and pulled up in front of their house. It would be great to thank them for what they'd done, but their windows were all dark. They'd probably been asleep for hours.

He would put the Harley's keys through their letter-box so Kitty could return them to her brother. And he'd call Jack tomorrow to tell him he'd been right. He needed the break. He was sure he'd be able to concentrate on his work much better because of it.

Oz sat on the Harley, listening to its engine cool and looking at the dark windows of Jack and Kitty's house. He remembered something Jack had confided to him, soon after his wedding.

"You know something I never expected about falling in love, Oz?" he'd said. "I love just sleeping with Kitty. I love hearing her breathe. And closing my eyes knowing she's the first thing I'm going to see when I open them again." He'd laughed like a man who couldn't believe his luck. "Never expected to hear me say I love sleeping almost as much as sex, did you?"

Oz looked away from the house, feeling as if he were intruding on his friends' happiness by being outside their window when they were blissfully asleep inside, together in their universe of two.

He needed to drop off the Harley, pick up his car, and go home and go to sleep. By himself.

So he could get up and go back to his real life tomorrow. By himself.

He realized he was staring at his hand holding the key to the motorcycle. He hadn't pulled it out of the ignition yet.

He turned it instead. Started the Harley.

It wasn't tomorrow yet. He could return the bike later. Tonight he wanted a little more of the fantasy.

Marianne and he had ridden south, so he went north this time. He rode up toward Freeport on Route 1, only seeing two or three cars. The night felt as if it belonged to him alone. But after half an hour, Oz turned around and headed back home. The fantasy wasn't working.

The Harley was a stunning machine. It responded to his every touch with perfect precision and awesome power.

And it felt like a stupid, inanimate pile of metal and rubber when he was on it alone.

He drove home. His house was dark, but he didn't bother to switch on any lights as he walked to the kitchen. He knew where all the furniture was, and there wasn't anybody else living in the big Victorian house to put anything where he'd trip on it.

When his sister Daisy had been living with him, he'd had to negotiate her cast-off shoes and textbooks all over the floor. But not anymore.

He opened the refrigerator and took out a bottle of water. For the sixty millionth time he saw the six-pack of diet soda that Daisy had left behind when she'd moved out a month ago, and for the sixty millionth time he thought he should bring it into the office because his receptionist would probably drink it.

And for the first time he realized he wouldn't bring

it into the office because he liked having the reminder of his sister's presence in his refrigerator. It made him feel as if there were someone around.

He wondered if Marianne drank diet soda.

She didn't need to; her figure was perfect. Then again, Daisy hadn't had to worry about that, either, but she still counted calories all the time.

He thought about Marianne's figure. Her long, slim legs wrapped around his waist from behind as they rode the motorcycle. Her breast in his hand, full and warm and throbbing with her heartbeat underneath. Her waist. Her bottom pressed against his lap.

The momentary sadness, a regretful look, almost, when she'd said how alone the lighthouse looked. And then her sexy smile, framed by her innocent dimples.

Oz realized he was standing staring into the refrigerator. And he was well on his way to a hard-on again.

He chuckled, swung the fridge door shut, and took a welcome drink of cool water.

Okay, it wasn't surprising he was reacting this way, he thought, heading for the stairs up to his bedroom. He'd been sublimating his sexual urges for…well, a long time. Repressed desires always reared up and grabbed you by the short and curlies when you least expected them.

To put it technically.

The moonlight was slanting through his bedroom window. He sat on his bed and pulled off the studded S and M boots, and then began the long process of unbuckling, unzipping, and unsnapping the pair of chaps.

He wondered how long it would take Marianne to take off his chaps. And what she'd say as she did it, in that sweet Southern accent. What surprises she'd come up with.

He shook his head. Her accent was sexy. Her body was sexy. And her surprises were sexy, too.

But he should stay away from her. He didn't need a woman with issues.

Problem was…her issues were sexy, too.

Oz stood up and kicked off the chaps and his jeans. She was daring, and yet she was innocent. She was confident, and yet she was lonely. She lived in a one-bedroom apartment above a bar, yet she had money and she stood straight and tall like a princess.

She was hot, teasing, incredibly responsive to his touch. And reluctant to actually have sex.

Oz threw off the ripped Harley Davidson T-shirt and went into his bathroom in his boxer shorts. He turned on the light and grimaced, catching sight of his fake tattoo. He snagged a washcloth from the side of the tub and scrubbed at it.

It didn't budge. How did you get these things off?

Marianne had liked it. And then she'd hated it.

It was as hard to remove as the memory of her touch on his skin.

He gave up scrubbing.

Marianne, he mused as he brushed his teeth, wasn't just a beautiful woman. She was an intellectual puzzle. Figuring out what made her tick would be a fascinating challenge.

As he reached into the bathtub to turn on the shower he caught a scent on his shoulder. Powdery, feminine. Pure.

Instantly he was back in the park, sitting on the grass, Marianne wrapped around him, his lips on her neck, her hands on his back, the wide, dark night all around them

When he was with her he felt wild, free, as if the whole world had opened up into a dizzying range of possibilities.

He turned off the shower. He didn't want to get rid of her scent just yet.

And, yes, that was irrational. But tonight, irrational just seemed like a good idea.

"Okay, Warren Webb, eat your heart out."

Marianne surveyed the drinks she'd lined up on the bar. A draft beer. A Southern Comfort and cola. A margarita on the rocks. A martini, shaken, not stirred. And a Shirley Temple.

She'd gone to bed last night discouraged, feeling that her new life was bound to be as much of a failure as her old life had been.

But with the morning had come optimism. Okay, so she'd chickened out on having sex with a total stranger. But that didn't mean she couldn't still learn some new tricks. She'd just gone about it the wrong way, that was all. She'd tried jumping off the high board before she'd even stuck one toe in the pool.

She'd start small, she'd decided.

So when she'd looked around her one-bedroom apartment, really looked at it in full daylight, she hadn't been dismayed by how poky and worn out it was. Or by the cracks in the plaster, or the stains on the walls, or the dust bunnies in the corners. And when the tiny shower cubicle in the bathroom had only been able to produce a trickle of lukewarm water, she'd only shivered a little and sang "Yankee Doodle" anyway.

She'd had enough of steaming hot showers and professionally decorated interiors. She was going to enjoy living in squalor for a while.

First, she'd learn to be a bartender. Maybe have a few late nights swapping jokes and flirtations with the clientele. Maybe buy some slutty high heels and paint her toenails candy-apple red. Maybe take up chewing gum and practice swearing and go out dancing somewhere.

She'd start small, and work her way up to something big. Like Oz.

Like someone gorgeous like Oz, but not with a doctorate in psychology, she amended.

She looked at the row of drinks on the bar and tried to think of another one she could make before Warren showed up. What else did people drink? Wine? Piña coladas? Harvey Wallbangers?

Marianne smiled. There was a whole universe of suggestively named cocktails just waiting for her to explore.

She rummaged around underneath the bar until she pulled out a slightly sticky copy of *The Bartender's Bible.* Typically of Warren, he'd dog-eared the pages with the sexiest-named drinks on them.

She found one with only three ingredients: vodka, Baileys, and Kahlua. That couldn't be hard. There were about a dozen bottles of vodka on the bar shelf, so she chose the one with the plainest label, figuring that'd be the cheapest, just in case she got it wrong. She measured it carefully into a glass filled with crushed ice. Then she poured in the Baileys.

The mixture immediately curdled into lumps.

Marianne checked the book. Was it meant to be a drink you had to chew?

Somehow she didn't think so. She tried pouring the Kahlua over it, but that didn't make it look any better.

Maybe a plastic umbrella or some fruit or something would help. She knelt down to search for garnishes under the bar.

She heard the door open and called, "Hey, Warren, check out your new drink special!"

"Are these all for you, or are you lining them up for your regular Sunday morning customers?"

It wasn't Warren. It was Oz.

Marianne stood up so quickly that her head spun. He was just on the other side of the bar, wearing jeans, a flannel shirt and his leather jacket, his blond hair wild, his smile digging lines in his cheeks.

She stepped back. She thought she'd been attracted to the bad-boy look of him. But he wasn't wearing chaps or a fake tattoo or a muscle shirt, and he looked absolutely delectable anyway.

"Dr. Strummer." She fought to keep her voice calm and honey-sweet. "How nice to see you again. Can I get you a drink?"

"It's early in the day for alcohol," he said. "Besides, I like my beer with more beer in it." He picked up the glass of draft beer she'd poured. It was more than half foam.

"The draft tap is tricky," she said. "It spat at me."

Oz nodded. "What's that? Some sort of cheese?" He pointed to the drink she'd just mixed, and narrowed his eyes. "In…chocolate sauce?"

"It's a Screaming Orgasm," she said, holding up her chin. She was not going to be embarrassed about saying "screaming orgasm" just because she'd nearly had one in his arms last night.

His smile got wider, and she felt herself flushing a

little. "So what can I do for you, Dr. Strummer?" she asked.

"I'd rather you called me Oz. You're not one of my patients." He sat down on one of the bar stools across from her.

"You're right. I'm not. So what can I do for you, Oz?" She made sure she asked the question exactly the same way as she had the first time: distant, polite, and with a charm that would freeze beer.

She watched him consider the other drinks on the bar. He picked up the last one and sniffed it. "Shirley Temple?"

She nodded.

Oz put one of the straws in his mouth and took a sip. Marianne, despite herself, stared at his lips around the straw. They were so well-formed. Sculpted. Sensual.

Last night, they'd been on her skin. Around her nipple.

She crossed her arms over her chest, but couldn't stop looking at his mouth. His neck, moving as he swallowed.

"It's good," Oz commented.

"I've got a way with ginger ale and grenadine," she said. "You haven't told me what you want yet."

Except for last night. He'd told her exactly what he wanted last night.

"I've come to take you out for lunch," he said. "I asked you yesterday, remember?"

"I remember. I said no."

"You didn't actually say no. You got distracted by my real identity and started flinging accusations around." He leaned back on his bar stool and smiled at her. "So I chose to take that as a yes."

Marianne picked up the curdled Screaming Orgasm and dumped it into the sink. "I'm working," she said.

"The sign on the outside of the bar says you're not open until two o'clock. It's only noon."

"I'm learning how to make drinks."

"So you can already make Screaming Orgasms, beer, and Shirley Temples. The Sex on the Beach can wait until later." She caught his eyes as he said that.

Oz stood up suddenly, reached over the bar, and caught her wrist in his hand. "Marianne, I like you. I want to get to know you better. Please come out with me."

Just the gentle grip of his fingers on her skin was enough to send a thrill of desire through her body. She bit her lip.

"I'm so attracted to you I can't think straight," he said quietly. "And I doubt that you bid all that money on me because you liked my chaps."

"No," she said. "It wasn't just the chaps." She couldn't breathe properly. "But, Oz, I—"

"I'll respect your limits," Oz said. His hazel eyes were steady on hers. "Come on, Marianne. Come out with me. Take a risk."

And just like that, he had her. A supremely sexy man telling her to do exactly what she'd decided to do anyway: take risks. She nodded.

For a man who'd appeared so doggone confident from the minute he'd walked into the bar, he looked hugely relieved at her answer.

The Harley was parked outside the front door of the bar, exactly where it had been last night. Marianne stopped. "I thought the bike wasn't yours," she said.

"It isn't. It belongs to a friend. I decided to borrow it for the weekend." Oz ran his hand over the leather seat. "I hadn't been on a motorcycle for eight years before last night. That was why I stalled it." He smiled at her, that little-boy-being-bad look. "I'd forgotten how much I loved riding."

"Why do you love it?" she asked, before she remembered how it had felt like sexual foreplay.

Oz was obviously reading her mind. "Besides having a beautiful woman wrapped around me?"

Marianne managed a nod.

"The freedom," Oz said. "You know how I told you about sneaking into the park to get away from my family? It's the same thing. Only a lot faster."

"What do you need to feel free from?" she asked.

"Responsibility. My job. My life. Who I am." He looked at her, his head tilted in the way she was learning he did when he was thinking. "Don't you feel the need for something similar?"

Exactly, she thought. "Maybe," she said. "Don't you like who you are?"

"I like who I am. But sometimes I want to be someone else." Oz bent down beside the Harley and picked up two helmets she hadn't noticed before. "I got these this time. It's more fun not to wear them. But this way the bugs don't get into your eyes."

Marianne put hers on. "Where are we going?" she asked, not sure if he could hear her through the helmet. Her voice sounded both muffled and loud in her ears.

"Do you trust me?" Oz asked.

She shrugged. Strange—last night, when she hadn't known who he was, she'd trusted him completely. Today she knew his real job and what he really looked like and she felt much more wary.

"Better question," he said. "Do you trust my driving?"

"Yeah. Don't stall it though."

"Your wish," said Oz, pulling on his own helmet, "is my command."

Was it? she wondered as she got on the back of the Harley behind him. He'd said he'd respect her limits. But did he mean it? Would he keep his perfectly shaped doctorate in psychology's nose out of her head?

On the other hand, what about her other wishes? Like the fact that as she wrapped her arms around his waist again she wanted to unbutton his flannel shirt and feel his bare stomach under her hands? Like how she wanted to stand up on the bike and bury her face in the crook of his neck, feel his pulse, smell his scent, as she'd felt and smelled it last night?

Were those wishes his commands, too?

Whoa, girl. Take it one step at a time, remember.

Well, maybe two.

"Drive it fast again," she said.

CHAPTER SIX

THEY pulled up at a roadside picnic area, and Oz cut the engine. Marianne pulled off her helmet and tumbled off the motorcycle exhilarated, laughing, panting. Her legs buckled and she stumbled, but then Oz was off the bike and he caught her in his big hands.

Close to him again. She curled her fingers around the leather arms of his jacket and looked up at him. His cheeks were pink and his hazel eyes twinkled.

"Do you always get weak-kneed after riding big thrusting machines?" he asked.

"Do psychologists ever get tired of Freudian remarks?" she shot back.

"Not really. It's one of the perks of the job." He ran his palm over her hair, smoothing it. "I was right."

"About what?" She was standing upright, but she still didn't feel very steady.

"Riding the Harley is much, much better with you on it."

"I like it," she said. What an understatement. She'd been whooping again as they rode. Joy had bubbled out of deep inside her and she hadn't been able to keep it in.

"Would you like to know my deepest, darkest

secret?" Oz asked her. His eyes were steady on hers; his voice had taken on that low, rumbly tone. As it had last night. She felt a shiver go through her, even though she was warm, and she nodded.

"I've had two speeding tickets in the past two years," he said. "Both of them on deserted stretches of road in my car." He tipped back his head and let out a long, laughing breath. "There. Nobody knows that except for you, me, and the Maine State Police."

"Ooh," she teased. "Dr. Strummer has a secret life of crime."

"Yeah. I'm hoping lunch will be good enough to keep you from blackmailing me." He turned to the Harley, opened up a saddlebag on the back, and took out a canvas bag that he slung over his shoulder. "There's a good spot down here for a picnic."

He took Marianne's hand and led her down a path going into the woods by the side of the road. The leaves had fully changed color, and the sun shone through them, orange and yellow and bright, startling red.

"I'm glad to find out you're not such a paragon of virtue after all," she said. Trying to keep her voice light, despite the touch of his fingers on hers, reminding her of them touching her in other places. Reminding her of just how sinful Oz could be.

Oz laughed. "I bet last night you thought I'd done a lot worse than speeding tickets." He hooked a pile of leaves with his foot and sent it showering over her. They whispered through the air, dry and delicate, like flakes of sunshine.

"No," she protested, though of course she had. She felt herself blush. "I'm not really a complete idiot who judges people on appearances."

Or was she?

She'd always assumed, herself, that people were judging her that way.

"I didn't mind being thought of as wild and reckless," Oz said. "I liked being your fantasy."

He stopped walking and reached toward her with his other hand, and Marianne caught her breath.

He was going to take her in his arms again. Kiss her. Start doing everything that made her want to rip off all her clothes and beg him to put his hands all over her.

His fingertips touched the front of her jacket. Marianne looked down and realized that he was just brushing off a vibrant orange leaf that had stuck to her. It fluttered to the ground, but Oz's hand didn't move. He kept his fingers there, just above the swell of her breast, right where he could surely feel the pounding of her heart.

"Could I still be your fantasy now?" he asked. The thumb of the hand that held hers stroked the inside of her wrist. Two touches, neither of them overtly sexy, both of them sexy as all get-out.

"You mean despite the Ph.D. and the steady job?" She couldn't quite look up into his face. If she saw his mouth, she'd want it. She remembered the taste of him, and licked her lips.

"It's worse than that," Oz said. "My father's a minister and my mother teaches Sunday school."

Marianne burst out laughing. "Oh, my gosh," she spluttered, "and I thought they called me Goody Two-shoes."

"They call you Goody Two-shoes?"

Oz's voice was curious. Marianne glanced into his eyes—keen, hazel, intelligent.

"Not since I got kicked out of the Brownies," she

lied. She turned away from him, pulling her hand from his, and started walking down the path again. Oz kept pace.

"So what made you decide to be a psychologist?" she asked, to change the subject. "Do you like analyzing people?"

"I like to understand people." Oz spoke genially, as if he hadn't noticed, or didn't care, that she'd brushed him off. She felt unreasonably nettled.

"And why is that? Does it give you some power over them?"

"Power?" Oz frowned. "It's—I—no, of course not." She heard him clear his throat. "If I understand people, I can help them."

"Is this your patients, or everybody?"

"Everybody. Including myself."

Marianne realized that if she told Oz about her past, he'd understand it. Her lonely upbringing, the way she'd felt her parents' love was conditional, her anorexia—he'd understand it all. He probably dealt with people with eating disorders all the time.

As his patients.

Did she really want him to consider her that way?

And yet, the idea of being understood. Of admitting her mistakes to someone who she knew wouldn't automatically reject her. It was seductive. Almost as seductive as Oz himself.

"Can I ask you something weird?" Oz said suddenly.

"What?"

If he asked her about her past, what would she choose to do?

"Can I pick you up?"

She looked over at him, confused.

"I mean—not pick you up as in feed you lots of lines and flirt with you and take you home with me. Though I'd like to do that, too. I mean literally. Like I did last night on the stage." He took his hands out of his pockets and looked down at them, and then at her. "I like holding you. I've been thinking nonstop about having you in my arms again."

She suddenly found it very difficult to breathe. His words seemed to grab her by the waist and to trail, like hands, up and down her body at the same time, stroking all her nerve endings into a frenzy of wanting.

She nodded. It was about all she could do.

"Great." In a single, swift movement, as if he'd been planning it, Oz swept her up, one arm under her knees, the other around her waist. She clung to his neck and breathed in his smell, shampoo and leather and man.

He was so strong and so gentle. Marianne had never been attracted to gentle men before, she realized. Jason had been strong, but he'd been rather abrupt in his movements. Decisive. As a future chief executive should be. Her other boyfriends had been athletic, usually—golfers, swimmers, captains of the football team. But Oz was assured in his strength, comfortable in his body, in a way that none of them had been. And he was careful of the way she was smaller than him.

In his arms, she felt precious, without even doing anything.

Oz's cheek brushed against her temple and she heard him inhaling. His hands tightened on her waist and her thigh.

"I thought how I felt last night was a temporary madness," he said. "I thought I'd wake up this morning and I would be back to normal. But when I woke up I still felt the same way." His voice, low in his chest, vibrated through her as the Harley did every time she was on it. "All I could think about was seeing you again. I started planning ways that I could touch you."

She saw his eyes sweep over her body and then come back to meet hers. "I've never met someone and felt so instantly attracted before," he said. "I didn't even know your name and I knew I wanted you, as soon as I saw you on the bar. I still don't know anything about you, and I still can't get you out of my head. It's completely irrational. I don't understand it."

"I don't understand it either," Marianne said. Because she wasn't supposed to feel this way about Oz, anymore, now that she knew he wasn't the type of guy she'd decided to want. But she wanted him, all right. Her right breast rubbed against his chest and she felt her nipples tighten almost painfully.

Oz started walking, carrying her. "I've trained for years to have insight into things like this, and it's not helping me. I feel like a caveman in mating season."

She couldn't help laughing, though that did little to relieve her sexual tension. Especially since the movement pressed her breast tighter against him. "What a waste of a finely tuned mind."

"Tell me about it. Do you think it's pheromones? Something about your scent that stimulates my limbic system?" He bent his head to her neck, and inhaled deeply. The soft movement of air against her skin felt like a kiss.

"Limbic system?" she managed.

He straightened and nodded. "The deep part of the brain that controls emotion and responds to scent." He frowned. "There has to be some chemical explanation of why I want to tear off your clothes right here in the middle of a public picnic area, in full daylight, and make love to you."

"I—" Her voice was strangled.

"And you feel the same way." He was walking, but his eyes burned into hers. "I can feel your heart beating against my chest. You're either excited, or you're scared. You're not scared of me, are you, Marianne?"

Scared to doggone death. How could he make her feel like this—breathless, brainless, a bundle of throbbing desire?

"Little old me?" she replied, taking refuge in sassiness. "Scared of the son of a preacher man?" She sang the last words and tossed her head.

She watched him smile, his full lips parting to reveal his strong white teeth.

"Here we are," he said, and stopped walking.

They were at the bank of a river. Water so dark blue it was almost black rushed over and around granite boulders, frothing white in the sun. She'd been so wrapped up in talking with Oz she hadn't even heard it. The trees around them were alight with autumn, leaves the color of flame against the dark green backdrop of the pines.

Oz set her on her feet, keeping his arm around her shoulders. They stood on a flat gray rock by the river. "Do you want some lunch?"

She wanted several things. Lunch wasn't one of them.

She nodded anyway. Lunch was safe. Safer than Oz's hands all over her, his mouth kissing hers, his hard, muscular body pressed against her. Lunch, she could keep control of.

Oz pulled her gently down to sit beside him on the rock, and tucked her underneath his arm. The granite was warm from the sunlight, glittering with flecks of mica. He unslung the saddlebag from his shoulder, opened it, and took out two foil-wrapped sandwiches.

"I've got peanut butter and jelly, or cheese." He held out the sandwiches to her, an apologetic expression on his face. "I haven't had any time to buy groceries lately."

"Peanut butter is fine," she said. She took it from him, her fingers brushing his and sending a shiver down her spine.

The colors around her so bright, the rock beneath them sparkling. It was as if she were the princess in some sort of fairy tale and had just been awoken to life. Oz held her, casually, not sexually, and yet she could feel in the tension of his body that he was restraining himself.

"What would a psychologist call your changing the subject like that?" she asked, unwrapping the foil with clumsy fingers. "From sex to peanut butter?"

"I'm sure a literal-minded clinician could connect the topics and diagnose a rather interesting kink." He unwrapped his own sandwich, but made no move to eat it. "But the real reason is because I'm trying desperately to distract myself."

He let out a long breath, and looked up at the bright blue sky.

"And this doesn't make sense to me," he said. "Purely physical lust can't be this strong. If it could be, I should've reacted this way to any number of women in my lifetime. And I've wanted women before, but not like this. You're different." His eyes, more green than hazel in this light, pierced her. "Why are you different, Marianne?"

"I don't know."

Yes, she did. All her life she'd been different. The girl with the richest family in the county, with the servants at home, with the doll's face and the doll's clothes. As she'd grown older she'd known that other kids had been intimidated by her name and her family, the fact that she'd got straight As in every subject, the way she'd been able to talk seriously with adults about grown-up things. She'd understood it, but it had still hurt. The only friend she'd ever felt comfortable with had been Warren, but she'd been kept too busy to see him much. And then he'd left Webb to find his own life.

Boys had asked her out. She'd been rich. She'd been Webb County Cotton Queen. She'd only chosen the ones her parents would approve of, and necked with them in their cars, never allowing them to go further. She hadn't lost her virginity until she was twenty and safely away at Duke. And she'd become engaged to Jason, the second man she'd ever slept with in twenty-five years.

Marianne was different, all right. She was practically a freak.

She took a bite of her peanut butter sandwich, chewed it furiously, and swallowed. At least she could eat, now. She wasn't freakish that way anymore.

"I think there's a reason," Oz said. "I think if I got to know you, I'd understand why I feel this way." He bit into his own sandwich, as if what he was saying was merely conversational, instead of probing, devastating, heart-accelerating. "Will you tell me about your past, Marianne?"

His arm was still looped around her shoulder. His hand toyed with the strands of hair that had escaped her ponytail in front. Even that little touch was thrilling.

She thought about how open he was about his desire for her. *I want to tear off your clothes right here in the middle of a public picnic area, in full daylight, and make love to you.*

If she told him about her past, he'd understand her. But he wouldn't look at her the same way anymore. He wouldn't see her as a mysterious, exciting woman. He'd see her as a woman with problems. A clinical case.

"What, you want to know why I got kicked out of the Brownies? I think you're a little bit of a pervert, Dr. Strummer." She took a big bite of her sandwich. If the peanut butter stuck her mouth shut, she wouldn't be tempted to talk, to share herself with him, to open up at last.

She saw the beginning of a frown between his eyebrows. "Okay. Can we talk about your present instead?"

The man was probably the cleverest person she'd ever met, and that was saying something. He had a plan; she could tell. And peanut butter probably wasn't going to help her. "Go ahead and talk," she said. "Let's see how smart you are."

Again, Oz ate some of his sandwich before he spoke, as if he were being casual instead of calculating. "You're not a bartender. You've never done it before."

"I'm learning."

He raised his eyebrows. "Your drinks look like cheese."

"Hey, it's not my fault if you don't know what an orgasm looks like." She shoved the rest of her half-sandwich in her mouth and chewed defiantly.

"Okay. You came all the way up here to train to be a bartender. Don't they have bars where you come from?"

"Didn't like any of them. I hate country music," she shot back.

"You've come from the Deep South to the most Yankee state you could find. Maine politics, Maine weather, Maine accents—they're all radically different to what you grew up with. Is that why you came here?"

"I wanted to try new things," she said.

"Are you going to stay in Maine?"

She'd been firing back answers, but on this question, she paused. "I don't know."

"You haven't thought that far ahead."

"I don't need to."

Oz took a bottle of water from his bag. "I've only got one of these. Do you mind sharing?"

She shook her head and took the bottle. The water was delicious and much cooler than she was. She handed it back to Oz and waited for another onslaught of questions. These ones, she could deal with. She wasn't ashamed of her decision to come to Maine to start a new life.

Instead of asking another question, he put the water bottle to his mouth and drank. Marianne couldn't tear her eyes away. She'd just touched that plastic with her lips, and now his lips were open around it. Tasting the water as he'd tasted her with his kiss, last night. The water was flowing over his tongue, his white teeth, down into his beautiful body where it would help his heart to beat, help his blood to flow to every one of his gorgeous muscles.

She felt herself melting all over again.

He lowered the bottle and wiped his mouth with the back of his hand.

How could such a simple gesture be so devastatingly

sexy? She shifted herself slightly on the rock, feeling altogether too warm, and bit into her sandwich again.

"Marianne, I'm watching you eat that sandwich and all I can think about is how I want to kiss you and find out how much sweeter peanut butter tastes in your mouth." He ran his free hand through his wild hair. "Maybe I do have some peanut butter kink after all."

"If that's true, I probably have a water bottle kink," Marianne admitted.

He glanced at the bottle and smiled.

"It's not a rational way to behave, is it?" he said, gently. "It's incredible. I've never felt anything like it before. But it can't be real, Marianne. Real relationships aren't based around not knowing anything about someone except for how much you want them. I want to share everything with someone who's not going to leave."

"I never said I wanted a relationship," she said. "I just bought you for a date, remember?"

"No, it's very clear that you don't want a relationship. You came up here running away from something."

She opened her mouth to protest, but he overrode her.

"You can deny it, but it's obvious to anybody who knows how to look. And people who run away always find their problems catching up with them. They have two choices when that happens: they keep on running away, or they go back to where they started. Either way, you're not going to stick around for long."

Marianne's mouth dropped open still further. She scrambled to her feet, suddenly furious.

"Hold on, mister. You just said you don't know anything about me. Just because you have some letters after your name it doesn't mean you can predict every little thing I'm going to do."

His expression, as he looked up at her, was infuriatingly self-assured. "Again, you're angry at me for no reason. I think I've hit a truth you're not comfortable about acknowledging."

She clenched her fists. "I'm not comfortable being here, period, if you're going to try to read my mind. I left home because I wanted to start a new life, and that's just what I'm going to do. Whether you think I can or not."

He stood. "And how are you going to be a whole new person when you're running from who you are in the first place?"

Her heart was hammering in her ears. "By doing exactly what I want, for a change," she said, not knowing what she was saying, not caring, hearing her voice loud and angry. "By doing stupid things without thinking about the consequences. By—by doing stuff like this."

And without even planning it, she had jumped forward, and grabbed Oz's head in her hands, and kissed him, hot, hard, and wild.

CHAPTER SEVEN

AND right away, again, it was out of control. The minute Marianne had Oz in her arms, the minute her lips touched his, she wanted all of him. Everything. She wanted to burrow under his clothes, tear them from him, explore every inch of his body she knew was golden, smooth, hard. She wanted him to fling her down right there on that rock in plain daylight and she wanted to open her legs to him and for him to push inside her.

She'd never wanted a man so badly. He'd been right, what he'd said.

It wasn't just lust. It was…something else.

But whatever else it was, it was lust too.

Her fingers were in his hair, curled tight, pulling. And his hands captured her hips, held them hard against him. He kissed her back. As if a wall between them had been suddenly torn down and they were right back where they had been last night: two strangers, united by an inexplicable feeling for each other.

Except they weren't strangers anymore. And the feeling was stronger.

She put her hands on his shoulders and pushed back from him. They stared into each other's eyes, panting.

His were bright and clear in the sunlight. She knew hers were wide.

And probably shocked. She felt shocked.

"I just yelled at you," she gasped.

"I noticed."

"I—don't yell at people."

"You do now."

She stared at him, her breath coming hard and fast, and tried to remember if, before she'd met Oz, she'd ever gotten so angry at anyone.

She'd been mad at Jason when she'd split up with him. But that had been cold anger, more like disdain as she'd seen the truth. Nothing like the hot passion that had flamed through her just now. That had turned into another kind of hot passion as soon as she'd touched Oz.

It was against every way she'd ever been taught how to behave.

Her skin tingled. Her blood felt alive in her veins. Every breath of air was vital, sweet, full of life and color.

This was exactly what she'd left home to feel.

Oz touched her lips with his finger. She wanted to open them, taste his skin with her tongue, feel even more alive.

"I can't do this," he said.

She couldn't help it. She closed her lips around the blunt tip of his finger, tasted salt and skin, and heard his breathing become harsher.

He pulled his hand away, a crease between his eyebrows as if he were in pain.

"I don't want something temporary," he said. "No matter how wonderful it feels."

"I want to feel wonderful," she whispered.

She wanted to *feel*. Plain and simple.

For a heartstopping moment, his head inclined to hers again. He was so close she felt his breath feather her cheek.

Something rang loudly.

They froze, and it rang again.

"My phone," Oz said, and he straightened and pulled a cell phone from the pocket of his jacket. He glanced down at it, his finger on the "off" button, but then he paused.

"Sorry, Marianne, I've got to take this," he said, and turned away from her. Marianne wrapped her arms around herself. His phone was obviously more important than her.

"Daisy," he said into the phone. "What's wrong, sweetheart?"

Marianne felt a painful and completely unnecessary stab of jealousy. She tightened her arms and lifted her chin. Of course a gorgeous hunk like Oz would have women dripping off him.

Then she remembered: Oz had told her last night that his youngest sister was called Daisy. The pang didn't quite go away with the realization, though.

His voice sounded so…patient. Tender.

"Calm down," he was saying. "Daisy, honestly, it's going to be fine. Trust me. Okay, stop crying and tell me what's the problem."

To keep busy, she knelt and started to tidy up the picnic things. It was good that the phone had rung, before she'd become so carried away she'd forgotten that she couldn't get involved with this man.

"Okay. I'll be there in ten minutes, tops. Hold on." Oz turned off the phone. "Marianne, do you mind coming somewhere with me? I'll take you home after, but my sister's having an emergency."

She frowned. “Is she all right?”

“She’ll live. She’s a little bit dramatic.” Oz knelt beside Marianne. “Marianne, I’m sorry.” He held out his hand toward her, and then appeared to think better of it, and brought it back.

“Just stay out of my head, Dr. Strummer.” She didn’t dare look at him when he was this close, in case something flared up between them again. She wasn’t sure which one was scarier: the passion, or the anger.

“I’m not sure I can, if I keep on seeing you,” Oz said.

She stuffed the water bottle into the canvas bag and stood. “Let’s go make sure your sister is okay,” she said, and headed down the path toward the Harley.

The motorcycle ride wasn’t any less intense, Oz wasn’t any less incredible, but Marianne wasn’t doing any whooping.

She’d decided this morning not to have anything more to do with Oz. She’d known as soon as she’d seen the “Dr.” in front of his name. She shouldn’t be bothered that he didn’t want to see her anymore.

What, after all, had changed? Just because they’d eaten a couple of sandwiches together?

She was so caught up in her thoughts that she was startled when the motorcycle slowed and stopped. She took her arms from around Oz and pulled off her helmet. They were in the parking lot of a mini-mall.

One of the doors of one of the shops burst open. “Oz!” cried a voice, and Marianne blinked.

A petite blonde woman was running toward them, wobbling in high heels, holding up the skirt of the ugliest wedding dress Marianne had ever seen.

* * *

His sister looked as if she'd been fighting a white satin balloon. And lost.

"What on earth are you wearing?" Oz asked, and then winced as he saw Daisy's face dissolve into tears.

"I know!" she wailed. "It's awful! And I can't make them listen to me!" She flung herself into his arms.

He patted her head soothingly. "Shh, it'll be fine." He looked over at Marianne, who was staring at them. "This is my sister Daisy," he said to her. "She's trying to plan her wedding."

"I can see," Marianne said, nodding slowly, not taking her eyes from Daisy's disastrous dress.

"I'll have to call it off," Daisy said into his chest. "I can't get married in this."

"You don't have to call it off, sweetheart. There must be some other dresses in the shop." He looked doubtfully at the masses of white satin enveloping his sister's slender body. "Unless that one ate them all."

She sobbed.

Marianne came around the side of the Harley and put her hand on Daisy's shoulder. "Come on, hon. It's a bad dress. But we can do better." She shot Oz a look that was the direct opposite of the honeyed voice she was using to speak to his sister. "You're not helping her with the dress-eating comments," she muttered.

Oz lifted his hands helplessly.

Daisy looked up, wet-eyed, from his chest. "Who are you?"

"I'm Marianne. And I might not know a lot of things, but I know how to shop. Come on back inside the store and tell me what you want." She put her arm around Daisy's shoulders and led her to the door. Oz followed, suddenly feeling unnecessary.

Within seconds, the two women were deep in conversation and using words he'd never heard of. Within minutes, they were flipping through the racks of white and ivory dresses, pulling some out to look more closely at, discarding others, totally absorbed in their search. He watched them. Daisy had stopped crying and was wiping mascara from beneath her brown eyes while nodding in agreement to something Marianne was saying. Marianne was holding the skirt of a dress, feeling the rich silk between her slender fingers. Her touch was sure and competent. He remembered how she'd grabbed him, not twenty minutes ago, and kissed him.

"Are you the groom?"

He pulled himself out of his reverie and looked down at the shop assistant beside him, a short gray-haired lady. "No, it's my sister who's getting married," he told her.

"Well, it's nice your girlfriend came to help her," the assistant said. "She was getting herself all wound up before, poor dear. Wouldn't take my advice."

"That's my sister for you," he said. He didn't bother to mention that Marianne wasn't his girlfriend. And wouldn't ever be.

"Oz!" Daisy called, and he went down the aisle of dresses to where they were. Maybe they needed his help.

"Here," Marianne said, handing him an armful of plastic-wrapped dresses. "Hold these while we find some more. We're going to try on a few styles to see which one your sister likes best."

He took the dresses and stood, feeling like a glorified coat hook, while they worked their way down the rack. Daisy rounded the corner and Marianne turned to him.

"Why is she doing this alone?" she asked him in a

low voice. "Why isn't your mother or one of your sisters with her?"

"She's had an argument with them," he told her. "They think she's getting married too young. So she's not talking to them."

Marianne's brow furrowed. "How old is she?"

Daisy popped her head back around the dresses. "I sort of like this pouffy one over here, Marianne," she said, and disappeared again.

"She's twenty," Oz whispered. "Just."

"Was she a cheerleader?"

Oz nodded.

"That explains a lot," Marianne said, and stepped closer to Oz. "We have to get her away from the pouffy dresses," she mouthed.

He nodded again.

They went around the corner and saw Daisy holding up something that looked even more balloon-like than the dress she had on. Except this one had giant bows on it.

He opened his mouth and tried to find something tactful to say, but Marianne beat him to it.

"Hon, that is beautiful, but I am betting you anything you fall in love with the raw silk. Come and try these on, and if you don't find one you like, we'll try that one, okay?"

Her voice held hundreds of years of Southern graciousness, sweetness and comfort and an unmistakable edge of authority. He watched his stubborn-as-grass-stains sister agree with her and teeter off happily to the changing rooms.

He walked alongside Marianne. He felt very big and

very out of place in this room full of lace and satin. "You've done this before, haven't you?" he asked her.

"Gone shopping? Yes."

"Gone shopping for a wedding dress."

Marianne stopped and pulled another dress off the rack. He could tell she was only pretending to study it to deflect his question.

"Do you think Daisy's too young to get married?" she asked, after she returned the dress.

"She's still at college. She moved out of my parents' house and she moved in with me, and then she got engaged to Steve and she moved in with him. She hasn't had any experience of being on her own."

"So you think she's too young."

"I'm worried that she's channeling some of her fears about the relationship itself into anxiety about the wedding."

"You think she's too young, and you're not saying anything because you don't want her to stop speaking to you, too."

They'd reached the entrance to the dressing rooms. Marianne took the dresses from him and disappeared behind the curtain. "Try on the raw silk first," he heard her advising Daisy, and then she was back out with him.

Oz took her elbow and guided her behind a display of veils. "I'm not confronting Daisy, because she's going to do exactly what she wants no matter what I say. She's my baby sister. I practically brought her up myself. It'll kill me if she gets hurt. But she's old enough to make her own choices."

Marianne had been all sweetness with his sister, but with him, her blue eyes flashed and her plump bottom lip was pushed out. She disliked the idea that he might be judging his sister, he could tell. She was trying to hide her past, but she left clues all over the place.

"I think people should be allowed to make mistakes, don't you?" he asked gently, watching her for her reaction.

He saw her hitch in a small breath as some emotion seized her. Then she was back to business. "Okay, well, she can make mistakes if you say so, but she's buying a pouffy dress over my dead body."

What was it? What mistake hadn't Marianne been allowed to make in her past? Or what mistake had she made that she was still making herself pay for now?

She would never share that with him.

"Oz?" Daisy's voice was full of excitement, almost as she'd sounded when she was a little girl and she'd come to him after winning a prize at school, or the leading role in her dance recital. But not a little girl's voice anymore.

He and Marianne went back around the veils to look at her. And he stopped short before he'd taken three steps.

The dress was ivory, a lustrous color that made Daisy's skin glow. It had a tight embroidered bodice that clung to every curve of Daisy's figure and a slim, elegant skirt that swept out behind her.

"Oh, Dais," he said, "you look like a princess."

And all grown-up.

She smiled at him, smoothed her skirt with her hands, and beamed at herself in the mirror.

Oz stood there, surrounded by symbols of innocence and permanence, and wondered when his sister had started being an adult and stopped needing him anymore.

"What do you think?" Marianne asked.

"I love it," said Daisy. "I didn't like it on the hanger and I thought the material looked all nobbly. But it's—"

"Perfect," Oz finished for her. He went to her and hugged her and buried his face in her hair. Remembering when it had been baby-fine, and she had smelled of milk. He tightened his arms around her.

"Oz, you'll crush the dress," Daisy protested.

He let her go.

"It really is perfect," Marianne said. "You look stunning. Do you want to try on the other ones, just to be sure?"

Daisy clearly couldn't drag herself away from the mirror. But she bit her lip and nodded. Reluctantly, she turned and went back into her dressing room.

Oz looked at Marianne. She had excellent taste in wedding dresses. And knowing that only made him want her more.

"I need to talk with you in private." He grabbed her hand and pulled her through the open door of one of the other dressing rooms. It was big for a dressing room, with real walls and a chair in the corner. He shut the door after them.

And then realized that though the dressing room was big, it still felt very small when he was in it with Marianne. She was watching him in surprise, and he could see by her face that she was as aware of their proximity as he was.

He leaned against one of the mirrors and folded his arms over his chest. The position implied authority, which wasn't what he wanted, but if his arms were free he'd be too tempted to touch her.

"I have to explain something to you," he said. "So

you'll understand why I can't see you anymore, even though I really want to."

"Go ahead and explain," she said, folding her own arms, and looking spirited and adorable.

"I'm the oldest of six children. From the age of four I had to share my room and my toys and my books and my parents' love. My parents were busy with my father's ministry and with community work. And a lot of the time they felt that homeless people or mourning people or whatever were more needy than six healthy, intelligent children. I had to take care of my brothers and sisters. And I don't resent that, because my siblings are wonderful people and my parents meant well but it meant that I have never had anything for myself. Not even my time."

There was a wedding dress hanging on the hook behind Marianne. He remembered Daisy in her dress, and ran his hands through his hair.

"I was nine years old when Daisy was born and she was mine. I was her special big brother. I did everything for her. I used to come home from Harvard especially to see her ballet recitals when she was a kid. And now she's all grown-up, and I don't have anybody anymore."

Marianne's arms were still folded and her chin was still tilted up in an expression of defiance, but her eyes betrayed a more complex emotion. Wistfulness, almost.

"And so I can't keep on seeing you," Oz continued. "I need something and somebody permanent, Marianne."

Her lips tightened. Her chin lifted another half inch. "I see," she said. "Well, that's very logical. Do you think I can go help Daisy with her other wedding dresses, now?"

He stood aside so she could sweep past him, dignified and straight-spined.

Daisy was in front of the mirror again, but she was still wearing the raw silk dress. "I don't need to try on any others," she said, seeing them approach her in the mirror. "This is the one."

"I think you're right," said Marianne. "You have to go with your feelings for something like this. Either something's right, or it's not."

Was it his imagination, or was she saying something to him as well as to his sister?

Daisy turned and seized her arm. "Will you help me pick out a veil and shoes and everything? I know I've just met you, but you have great taste and you seem to know exactly what I like."

Marianne glanced at her watch. "Well, I have to get Oz to take me back to work right now. But I'd love to look at wedding things with you. Maybe next week?" She shot Oz a look. "I think I can manage to stick around that long."

Great. The woman he couldn't have was making friends with his sister.

Well, his sister and he had separate lives now. There was no reason for him to run into Marianne. He'd take her back to the bar, and endure the exquisite torture of her arms and legs around him one more time, and then he'd never have to see her again.

CHAPTER EIGHT

"So what's the big mystery?" Jack strode alongside Oz, rubbing his hands together. "We haven't been out together on a school night in ages. Tell me we're going someplace exciting."

"We're going to a bar." *Now he's going to tease me about working too hard,* Oz thought.

"A bar? At eleven o'clock on a Wednesday night? Whoa, there. What time do you have to get up tomorrow?"

"I have a patient at eight. I'll get up at six and work out."

"You are such a party animal. So why are we wasting your precious working time going to a bar?"

Oz walked along in silence for a while before he answered. "I've met someone."

Jack stopped dead on the sidewalk. "You've—Oz, that's great! Who'd you meet? Where'd you meet her? Wait—it was the Harley, wasn't it?"

"Yes."

Jack punched the air. "Ha! I knew it!" He slapped Oz on the back and beamed. "And you're taking me to a bar to meet her because you're absolutely crazy about her."

"I'm—well, I keep on thinking about her."

Understatement. He'd thought about Marianne, dreamed about her, tasted and smelled and felt the memory of her, every single moment for the past week and a half.

He'd returned the Harley to Kitty's brother Nick and gone back to his life. He'd tried to forget Marianne, because she wasn't what he needed. Patients, lectures, hours on the rowing machine trying to work this burning feeling out of his body. Trying to get back to normal.

He couldn't even remember what normal felt like anymore.

"Ha!" Jack shouted again. "I hate to say I told you so, but—" He threw up his hands. "What am I saying? I *love* to say I told you so. Finally, after all these years, Jack Taylor is right about something and Oz Strummer doesn't have a clue. I knew that when you found a woman it would hit you like a thunderbolt and you wouldn't know what to do about it. I told you so on my wedding day. Well, you're in luck, Dr. Strummer, because since meeting Kitty I am a bona fide expert on love."

Oz laughed. "Does Kitty agree with this?"

"She says I'm a gifted amateur. But I'm getting better every day." Jack raised one eyebrow at him. "So. You've fallen in love at first sight."

"I've told you before. I don't believe in love at first sight. Love is something that grows out of mutual knowledge and respect."

Jack snorted. "Uh-huh. And this is why you're so hot and bothered about all the other women you know and respect."

Oz turned the corner to the street where Marianne's bar was. He remembered the last time he'd been here: on the Harley, with Marianne wrapped around him. At the thought, a bolt of sizzling lust zapped its way from his pounding heart straight to his crotch.

It was an obsession. It was some sort of compulsive behavior, driven by his suddenly hyperactive libido. He should take up cold showers.

"I'm more than hot and bothered," Oz admitted. "My brain has been completely taken over by my gonads."

"That's excellent."

"No. It's very bad. I'm a wreck."

Jack nodded sagely. "Not going well, huh? What happened? Did you try to analyze her? Tell her what she was thinking?"

Oz set his jaw. "I was just trying to understand her."

"And what did she do?"

"She got angry. And then she kissed me."

Jack threw back his head and laughed. "This woman is great. I can't wait to meet her."

"Well, you're about to." They were at the glass door of the bar. The night was lit up with pink and blue neon. Oz's heart leapt up into his throat.

He was excited to see Marianne again. And scared. Because something had changed in how he felt about his life since he had met her.

Change is frightening. He told his patients that all the time, to reassure them that the fears they felt about getting well were normal. He'd always understood it intellectually, but never in his gut. Not as he understood it now.

I'm just going in to look at her, he thought. *Maybe talk to her.* He put one hand on the door to push it open. But he didn't.

"What are you waiting for?"

Oz looked at Jack, still not opening the door. "I probably won't like her as much as I think I do. I've probably been thinking about her too much and built her up in my fantasies into something she isn't. Have I ever told you Lacan's theories about the impossibility of desire?"

Jack shook his head. "Man, you have got it bad. Come on, I'm thirsty."

Oz took a deep breath and pushed open the door. "She probably won't even be here," he said, and then stopped.

She was behind the bar. He didn't even have to look around to find her. His gaze was drawn unerringly across the room to where she stood, her dark hair gleaming and loose around her face, her skin pale and pure, her eyes and her mouth lit up in a smile.

She wasn't smiling at him. She hadn't noticed him. She was wiping the bar with a cloth and talking to someone beside her, and Oz could hear the sweet drawl of her voice, like honey smoothing over his nerve endings. He could feel the skin of her cheek beneath his lips, and the warm swell of her hips beneath his hands. He could smell her feminine, powdery scent.

"Which one is she?" he heard Jack ask beside him, and Oz came back to reality.

There was loud music. They were across the room from Marianne. There was no way he could really have heard Marianne's voice or felt her skin or smelled her perfume.

"There's more than one woman in the room?" Oz muttered, and for the first time he noticed that Marianne was smiling at a man. Oz registered tallish, dark-haired, slim, good-looking, and his stomach immediately felt as if it were going to eat itself in jealousy.

"She's the brunette talking to Warren, right?" Jack said.

Oz looked again and let out a breath of relief.

Jack was in a casual group of young business owners with Warren. Oz had had a few beers with them, played a couple of pick-up games of football. He knew Warren was gay.

At the same time, he remembered Warren was Southern.

"They're both from South Carolina," he said to Jack. "I bet they've known each other before."

"Excellent," Jack said. "So if you want to know anything about Marianne, you could ask Warren. He's a good guy. Huge Marlon Brando fan."

Warren could help him understand her, and if Oz understood her he could figure out how to make her stick around.

Marianne looked up from the bar at that moment and straight at Oz.

His heart stopped. Actually stopped.

And her smile wavered, dropped from her face for a moment, and then returned, slow and sweet and sexy, digging her dimples in her cheeks.

She was the most beautiful sight he'd ever seen in his life.

"I can't ask Warren about Marianne," he said, hardly aware he was speaking aloud. "I couldn't betray her like that."

Jack whistled low. "You've definitely got it bad."

Oz strode forward through the room to the bar. The entire room had disappeared again; all he could see was her blue eyes, her pink lips, the graceful column of her pale throat, and her slender body, leaning with her hands on the bar.

"Hi," he said when he got to her. Then he breathed in.

It was as if her scent were oxygen, and he'd been deprived of it for the ten days he hadn't seen her.

"Oz," she said. His name from her mouth was a pleasure so great he nearly groaned. Her eyes held his. "I thought you'd decided to stay away from me."

"I thought so, too."

"Well, I'm not gone yet." She was teasing him. Not just with her words, but with the lift of the corners of her lips, her head tilted just slightly to one side. She wore low-slung jeans and a tiny, tight top that clung to her breasts and ended just above her belly button. The sight of her softly curved bare belly and hip made his mouth water.

He wanted to launch himself across the bar and wrap his hands around her bare waist and pick her up and put her on the shelf behind her and kiss her until neither one of them could breathe.

She cleared her throat. "So what can I do for you, Oz?"

"I don't think I should answer that question in a public place," Oz replied.

Her dimples deepened. "Maybe that would make it more exciting," she drawled.

Oz opened his mouth, wondering as he did what his libido would find for him to say, when Jack appeared beside him. "Hi, Marianne," he said, stretching his hand across the bar for her to shake, "I'm Oz's friend Jack. I've been looking forward to meeting you for a long, long time."

She folded her arms across her chest and looked at Jack's hand. "Jack," she said, her voice cool and sweet as iced tea, "how nice to meet you. I suppose you're wondering whether Oz owes you a beer."

Jack looked at her, his eyes wide, his hand still outstretched. He looked at Oz, and then back at Marianne, and his grin grew. "You saw my note on the condom box, didn't you? Saying Oz owed me a beer for every condom he used?"

"Yes, I saw it. And you'd better get your own wallet out if you want a drink."

She shook Jack's hand demurely, and then got down two glasses and walked to the beer tap.

Jack nodded, still smiling broadly. "I like her. She's beautiful, she's intelligent, and she's got a smart mouth."

"I'm glad you approve."

"Why haven't you gotten her into bed yet? Doesn't she like you?"

"I like him. And anything else is none of your business." Marianne slid two glasses of beer toward them and winked at Oz. He felt the blood charging away from his head straight to his groin.

"Sorry," he said to her. "My friend is obsessed with sex. I keep on recommending therapy, but—"

"My wife would be very upset if I were cured," Jack cut in smoothly.

The two glasses of beer were clear, amber, with a perfect half inch of creamy head on each one.

"You've learned how to pour beer," Oz said, surprised.

"I've learned how to do a lot of things," Marianne said, smiling that innocent-yet-wicked smile again. "Would you like to try one of my new improved Screaming Orgasms?"

Jack nudged Oz. "Did I mention I think this woman is perfect for you?"

"Excuse us," Oz said, and steered Jack away to a table in the corner. "Jack, stop it," he hissed as soon as they were out of earshot of the bar. "Marianne's not interested in commitment. You'll scare her off."

"I think it would take a lot to scare that woman off," Jack said, sitting down and taking an appreciative sip of his beer. "From the minute you walked in there were practically sparks flying off the both of you. It was like there were only two of you in the universe."

Oz stopped mid-drink. *A universe of two.* Those were the words he'd used to describe Jack and Kitty, who were so much in love with each other.

He put down his beer. The foam lightly lined the side of the glass, just as it was supposed to.

"Why were you surprised she could pour beer?" Jack asked, obviously following his gaze.

"Ten days ago she was the most incompetent bartender I'd ever seen." Oz couldn't help but search out Marianne again with his eyes. She was carrying a tray of drinks to a group of men two tables away. He could see now that she was wearing a pair of red high-heeled shoes. The toes were open and her toenails were polished bright cherry red. Her hips swayed as she walked, but she held the tray absolutely steady, balanced on one hand.

She reached the table and put the drinks down. Oz watched the men watching her. He could imagine the view they were getting down her snug top. He clenched his fingers on his glass.

"Hey, gorgeous," the man closest to her said, "what you doing after work?"

"I'm busy, thanks." She put the last drink down and tucked the tray under her arm.

"Give me a chance; I could give you a wicked good

time." He leered at her and wiggled his fingers in the air in an obscene gesture. "I got magic fingers."

Oz leaned forward in his chair, ready to move.

Marianne's face flushed pink. "No, thank you." She turned to go.

"Come on, sexy," the man called after her. "If I could see you naked, I'd die happy."

Oz stood up and took a step toward the table.

Marianne turned around. She narrowed her eyes at the man.

"Yeah, but if I saw you naked, I'd die laughing," she said, dripping sweetness.

The other men all laughed as she walked away, grinning. Oz watched her go back around the bar and punch one fist into the air.

"She isn't incompetent anymore," Jack observed.

"No," Oz agreed, settling back in his chair. "She's good."

Jack leaned forward on the table toward Oz. "So what I don't understand is why the two of you aren't knocking boots at every possible opportunity."

"Like I said. She's not interested in commitment."

"Don't jump the gun, my friend. How are you going to get her to commit to you if you're so worried she won't commit to you that you stay the hell away from her?"

"Good point," said Oz. "It's not just that, though. She has some issues."

"With you, I would've thought that's a good thing. You like people with issues—you've been my best friend for fourteen years."

"Marianne's different. She's been repressing her anger for a long time. And I don't know why, but she's been repressing her sexuality, too."

Jack looked from Oz to Marianne, and back to Oz. "Oz, if you're talking like that, you must be repressing your own sexuality. The woman is beautiful. You've clearly got the hots for each other. Why are you staying away from her and quoting all this bull about Tin Can's theories about the impossibility of desire?"

"Lacan," Oz corrected automatically.

But suddenly he knew why he'd brought Jack to the bar with him.

For as long as they'd been friends, Jack had been the one who'd made Oz do the crazy things. Oz loved Jack for himself, of course. But he knew it was no mistake he'd chosen a happy-go-lucky, feckless friend. Just as it had been no mistake that Jack had chosen a responsible, intellectual friend. When Oz had wanted to do something stupid and fun, he'd had Jack to blame for dragging him along; and when Jack had wanted to do the right thing instead of the fun thing, he'd had Oz to blame for lecturing him.

But Jack had had a conscience all along, as he'd discovered when he'd fallen in love with Kitty. And Oz had always had a fun side, too. It was just easier to challenge your comfort zones when you had someone else egging you on.

Tonight Oz was following the same old pattern, relying on Jack to make him do what he really wanted to do anyway.

Oz suddenly felt foolish.

"I knew you'd say that," he said to Jack. "Why did I need you to say it, instead of trusting my own emotions?"

Jack shrugged. "I guess it's the curse of second-guessing everybody else. You start second-guessing yourself, even when you know the right answer." He glanced at his watch. "Listen, Oz, I'm sorry, but I'm going to have to go. We've got a midnight screening of *Midnight Cowboy* at the Delphi."

Oz gazed at his friend. "Two years ago I never would have dreamed you would be this responsible business owner giving me good advice about relationships."

"We all change, Oz. Maybe it's your turn now."

Jack left, and Oz went up to the bar again. Marianne skipped up to him in her high heels. Her cheeks were flushed pink.

"Did you see that?" she asked. "Did you see me put that guy in his place? I rule!"

She put her hands up in the air in victory signs, and began to shimmy back and forth in time to the beat of the heavy metal song that was blaring through the speakers. "Oh, yeah, baby," she sang, "I rule, and I can dance to Metallica!"

Oz laughed. He reached over the bar, caught her hand, and twirled her around to the music. She spun around and around, then let go of Oz's hand and teetered in her heels. Oz leapt forward to catch her, but Warren was there first, and she fell into his arms, giggling and beaming at Oz.

Warren set her on her feet, his arm looped around her shoulders. "Dr. Oz," he said, his Southern accent a deeper version of Marianne's, "I sure hope you're gonna treat my cousin right after she paid three grand for you."

"Cousin?" Oz repeated as he saw Marianne instantly lose her smile and shoot Warren a warning look.

Okay. Warren is family. And he definitely knows something Marianne doesn't want me to know, he thought.

Probably perversely, he became even more determined not to ask Warren about Marianne's past.

"I'll treat her right," he said.

Marianne shrugged out of Warren's embrace and leaned against the bar. The movement pressed her breasts against her chest and deepened the V of her cleavage, but Oz was more interested in her face: the lingering lines of laughter, the sparkle in her blue eyes.

"What would you like?" she asked.

"Whatever you'd like to give me," he said, and held her eyes with his.

Like his statement about treating her right, it felt like a promise.

Slowly, her smile grew again. "What do you think, Dr. Strummer?" she asked, her voice teasing. "You up for a little fun with Portland's newest bad girl?"

Up for was right. Just the thought of a little fun with Marianne had his crotch rock-hard and throbbing. She might have been repressing her sexuality before, but right now she was the luscious little temptress who'd climbed up on the bar and bid three thousand dollars for a date. And truth be told, he liked the temptress side of her even more because he knew that it was only part of her and that the confident, sexy side hid a softer, more vulnerable side.

"What have you got for me?" he asked.

Marianne tilted her head to one side, considering. "We're closing up the bar in fifteen minutes. Think you can stick around?"

On a school night? He heard Jack's mocking voice in his head, but he didn't need Jack to encourage him. He could do what he wanted, without excuses. "Yes."

She leaned still further over the bar, close enough so her face was bare inches from his.

"How about a game of strip poker?" she asked.

CHAPTER NINE

THE bar was closed, the room was empty except for the two of them, the lights were low, the music on the jukebox was soft and sultry soul.

"I'm ready when you are," said Oz. He looked beautiful. His leather jacket was on the back of his chair; he was wearing a blue shirt that accentuated the broadness of his chest, and brown low-slung cords that clung to every muscle of his legs. He'd run his hands through his hair about a dozen times since walking into the bar—she knew, because she'd been watching him every minute since she'd spotted him—and it was sticking up all over the place.

Marianne stood in her siren-red high-heeled shoes holding a deck of cards, and the sexiest man in the known universe was waiting for her to deal out the hands and start stripping.

And it was at that moment that Marianne remembered she'd never played more than a hand of poker before.

She shuffled the cards from hand to hand.

"So are you a good poker player?" she asked, stalling for time until she figured out what she was going to do.

How was it possible that his smile made him even

sexier? "Good enough that I expect to see your underwear in two hands," he said.

Oh, dear.

She shuffled the cards again, not sure if this was to distract him, or to buy her time, or to keep her hands busy so that she wouldn't jump on him and tear his clothes off without having to bother with poker.

Her quick wits saved her. "You seem so sure of yourself. I'd hate to demolish your male ego by beating you so badly at a game you think you're good at. Why don't we choose another game instead?"

His smile got even wider. "You don't know how to play poker, do you?"

So much for quick wits.

"What would you rather play?" Oz asked.

Marianne racked her brain. What card games did she know? Her life hadn't exactly been full of leisure time for playing games. She used to watch her grandmother's bridge parties when she was a little girl, but she couldn't quite see the connection between a load of elderly ladies playing cards and drinking afternoon tea around a little table, and herself and this big manly man in a closed-up bar late at night thinking about getting naked.

"Er..." And then she remembered stolen childhood afternoons with Warren, in the den his mother let them make with the couch cushions and a few blankets. They'd sneaked cookies and told scary stories and once or twice they'd played cards.

"How about Go Fish?" she asked.

Oz bit his lip. She could see he was trying not to laugh.

"Strip Go Fish," he said, gravely. "Yes, I think that would remove any unfair advantage either one of us might have."

She sat down at the table and dealt out the cards.

"So, remind me of the rules of strip Go Fish," Oz said. "At what point do our clothes come off?"

"You need to get sets of four of a kind," she explained, laying each card she dealt precisely beside the other ones to make a perfect line. "If you need a card, you ask me if I have it in my hand. If I do, I give it to you. If I don't, I say 'go fish' and you draw a card from the pile."

"And take off an item of clothing."

"You catch on fast." She tapped the remaining deck on the table to make a straight edge, and then put it exactly in the middle of the table and picked up her hand of cards.

Her own hands were trembling slightly, and her palms were damp.

I have no need to be nervous, she told herself. *This is wonderful. I'm doing exactly the sort of thing I promised myself I would. And I'm having fun.*

As much fun as she could have when she was trying desperately to be somebody she wasn't.

Yet, she reminded herself. "Okay, I dealt, you go first," she said.

Oz focused with great concentration on the cards fanned out in his hand. "Hmm. This is the toughest decision I've made all day. Do…you have any jacks?"

"Go fish," she said.

He didn't move. Just looked at her.

"Aren't you going to take a card?" she asked.

"What do you want me to take off first?"

Everything. "Er…your shoes?"

So how come not half an hour ago she'd been the perfect bad girl—pouring drinks like a pro, being sassy to customers, challenging a hunk to strip poker—and now she could barely ask him to take off his shoes?

"And your socks," she added. That was better.

Oz smiled, and bent over in his chair. She watched him unlace his brown leather boots and toe them off, and then pull off his socks.

He had nice feet. Like his hands, they were finely sculpted, but strong-looking. And big.

"Is it true what they say about men with big feet?" she asked.

Oz caught her eye and grinned wryly. "You'll have to say 'go fish' a few more times and find out."

"That's the plan," she said airily, and examined her own cards, silently cheering herself for being so sassy. "Do you have any tens?"

He shook his head and held out his hand. "Go fish, and I'll take those pretty red high heels, please."

Sassy. Be sassy and seductive.

Deliberately, she stood up and took the few steps to Oz. She raised her foot, holding on to the table for balance, and gave it to him.

Her foot looked small in his hand. He cradled her ankle in his hand, and with the other slowly slipped off her shoe. Then he held her foot. One of his thumbs stroked her arch; the other stroked down the top of it to her toes.

Tingling shot up her leg. She held on to the table for dear life, trying to keep her balance while she discovered for the first time in her life that her feet were erogenous zones.

Carefully, Oz set her foot down. The hardwood floor felt cold under her heated skin. He held out his hand for her other foot, and Marianne gave it to him. Her knuckles were white from holding on to the table so tightly. This time he slid her shoe off even more slowly. She watched his face; it was a picture of concentration as he traced her foot with his fingers, touching each of her toes, following the bones upward to her ankle, running down the side to underneath.

If he was this thorough with her feet, what would he be like with other parts of her body?

She bit her lip and forced herself to keep from groaning.

He ran his thumb over the ball of her foot, just near the underside of her toes, and the sensation was so intense, so ticklish and yet so erotic, that her other leg trembled. Oz glanced up from her foot to her face, and smiled.

"You need to draw a card," he said and set her foot down. She practically staggered back to her chair, collapsed into it, and took a card.

"A ten!" she said, holding it up. "That's what I asked for. I get another turn."

"Excellent. Another chance to say 'go fish.'" He leaned back in his chair.

"Do you have any twos?"

"Go fish," he said promptly, not looking at his cards. "Your shirt, please."

Her shirt? "You didn't even check to see if you had any twos!" she protested, her heart racing and heat flooding through her.

"I have a very accurate memory." His smile grew. "For instance, I remember exactly how gorgeous you looked with your blouse unbuttoned the other night. I'm eager to see you without a shirt again."

The other night. When she'd been too chicken to have sex with him.

Well, she wasn't chicken anymore. She'd been working on it for over a week now.

Before she had time to let herself think, she grasped the bottom of her tank top and pulled it over her head and threw it on the floor behind her.

Her bra was red satin and lace—the same color as her high heels and her nail polish, and the most overtly sexy piece of lingerie she'd been able to find in the shop. She had a very brief pair of matching panties on underneath her jeans. Her new "bad girl" wardrobe had cost her all of her tips for a week. She looked over at Oz's face to see if spending the money had been worth it.

He was sitting absolutely still, staring at her. His mouth was slightly open. He didn't appear to be breathing.

And his gaze on her was like hands trailing over her skin. She felt her nipples harden, making stiff peaks beneath the satin bra, her breasts aching.

The money had been worth it, all right.

"As—" Her voice was hoarse, and she choked on the words and had to try again. "As good as you remember?"

Oz nodded slowly, his eyes not leaving her. "Better," he murmured.

She picked up her cards and looked at them in what she hoped was the nonchalant manner of a woman who'd spent hours playing cards in her bra in front of men. "It's your turn," she said.

"Do you have any aces?" he asked, still in a low and sexy voice, still not checking his cards.

She had three. But she was darned if she was going to be the only one sitting here without a shirt on.

Besides, bad girls probably cheated at cards anyway.

"Go fish. And please remove your shirt."

He unbuttoned his cuffs first. His wrists were perfect, strong and dusted with blond hair. She watched as he pulled his shirt from his cords and unhurriedly unbuttoned it.

And then he uncovered his chest, inch by inch.

First, the long triangle formed by the cords of his neck, the muscles of his shoulders, and his sharply defined collarbone. Then, the broad swell of his shoulders, and his pectorals, gleaming with silky hair, his small male nipples delectable in the range of textures and shapes. And then his firm stomach. Every muscle visible beneath his golden skin. The shallow indent of his navel, just exactly the right size for the tip of her tongue. And his hair subtly darkening in a line down his abdomen and disappearing beneath the waistband of his cords.

"Geez, Louise," she breathed, "how did you get a chest like that?"

"I used to be a ninety-eight pound weakling," he said, "so I joined the rowing team when I got to Harvard. And I've been spending a lot of time on the rowing machine lately. I seem to have a lot of excess energy." His crooked smile made her heart beat even faster.

He crossed his perfect arms over his perfect chest and regarded her thoughtfully. "Help me out with something, Marianne. I can't figure you out at all. You're the sexiest woman I've ever met; you're wearing sinful lingerie and you keep on saying these wicked things. But you challenged me to strip poker when you didn't even know the game. When I told you to take off your top you blushed. And if my ears weren't deceiving me, when I just took off my shirt you said 'Geez, Louise.'"

She should've practiced swearing when she was practicing pouring beer.

"I'm a complex person," she said.

"I've noticed. How did you become such a good bartender?"

"I practiced. A lot."

"You said you were Portland's newest bad girl. Have you been practicing that, too?"

The man was practically a mind reader. And it was difficult to concentrate on keeping up her new image when she was distracted by the sight of his golden-skinned chest. His arms were thick and corded. She noticed the fake tattoo was gone. He didn't have a lot of chest hair, just enough so that it would tickle her bare nipples, rasp against her breasts.

She swallowed. "Don't you like bad girls?"

"I like you. Which is why I want to know who you really are."

At his words her eyes suddenly stung, and she needed to blink hard.

When was the last time anyone had asked her who she really was? Had tried to look behind the image she was projecting to the real Marianne underneath?

And who was the real Marianne anyway?

She picked up her cards and looked hard at them.

The real Marianne was scared. The real Marianne was uncertain of everything. The real Marianne was the person who was so frightened by her own desires that she'd frozen when Oz had made them overwhelm her.

Given the choice, she'd rather be the bad-girl stereotype, who was brave, sassy, and knew exactly what she wanted.

"Do you have any queens?" she asked.

"Go fish."

She stood up and walked to the side of the table to

stand in front of Oz. Slowly, she unbuttoned the top of her jeans and drew down the zipper.

She watched Oz's eyes. They'd been on her face, but as she hooked her thumbs into her waistband and wiggled her hips to slide the tight jeans down her legs, his eyes dropped to the triangle of red satin she knew he could see being revealed.

He was an intellectual and a mind reader. But he was a man, too. And he looked absolutely hypnotized.

She took her time undressing, enjoying him watching her, reveling in this power she seemed to have when she acted this way.

Inch by inch her jeans crept down her legs, until they lay at her feet, and she pulled one bare foot from them and then the other, and stood in front of Oz wearing only her naughty red panties and bra.

Oz licked his lips. She heard him draw in a shaky breath.

He opened his mouth. Then he shut it.

"Dr. Strummer is speechless," she said. "This has got to be a first."

He didn't make a move toward her, only looked. And looked. She felt caressed. Admired. Powerful.

"Everything I can think of to say is a cliché," he said, finally.

"Say it anyway."

He ran his hand through his hair, adding to its wildness. "You're the most beautiful woman I've ever seen in my life."

She smiled.

Marianne had been told she was pretty from the day she was born. But it had never, ever sounded so good as when Oz said it.

"What else?" she asked.

"I'm only holding on to my rationality by a thread here." Oz swallowed. "My mouth is actually watering."

"That's less of a cliché." She tossed her hair back from her face, and deliberately reached forward and took a card from the deck on the table. The movement allowed Oz to see down the front of her bra. She watched him swallow again, and then she looked at her card.

Six of spades. Maybe her lucky card.

"Your turn," she said.

Again, he didn't check his hand, just kept on staring at her. "Do you have any sixes?"

Marianne put the six of spades facedown on the table. "Go fish," she said.

Oz stood up. It was her turn to stare, hypnotized, as he unbuckled his leather belt and unbuttoned the fly of his cords. He pushed them down his long, muscular legs and kicked them aside.

When he straightened up she had to take a step back.

He was wearing white boxer/briefs that outlined every single bit of him: narrow hips, powerful thighs. And the biggest erection she had ever seen.

It was long. It was hard. It was thick. It pointed straight up and slightly to the left and it was dangerously close to poking out of Oz's waistband. It strained the material of his underwear and as she stared she saw it jerk and lengthen still more.

"I don't think you need me to tell you what I'm thinking about," Oz commented.

She barely heard him. She was imagining, in full sensual detail, what it would feel like to go over and put her hand on his penis. How hot it would feel through the cotton of his shorts. How it would do that little leap into her palm, and how she would wrap her fingers around its girth. What Oz's groan would sound like as she gave him pleasure.

A bad girl would do it.

And yet it was such a blatant thing to do. It was so hungry, so insistent. So much like showing how weak she was in the face of her own desire.

And what if she did it, or started to do it, and she lost her nerve? As she had the first night with Oz?

It would be so much easier if Oz would just grab me, she thought, chewing on her lip, trapped between lust and fear. *If he would make the decision. If I could be what he wants me to be, tonight.*

And that was it. Her solution. She smiled, and stepped closer to Oz.

"What are you thinking about, exactly?" She made her voice sweet, low, drawing out the accent she knew he found sexy.

"It's no different than what I've been thinking about constantly since I met you," he said, his words ragged-sounding. "Making love with you. Repeatedly. Except right now my thoughts are a little more—urgent."

She stepped still closer and stood a bare inch from his body. She could feel the heat from his skin, hear his harsh breathing, smell his spicy scent.

"How urgent?" she asked, and went forward that last little bit. Her breasts brushed his chest through her lacy bra; his erection poked against her stomach, as hard and hot as she'd known it would be.

Touch me, she thought.

Oz closed his eyes. His deep breath closed the

distance between them even more, pressed her nipples more firmly against him, his erection harder against her.

Then he opened his eyes again and looked into hers. His gaze was hazel, clear, intelligent, and almost looked as if he were in pain.

"Is this what you really want?" he asked. "To have sex for the first time together in a bar, on a table, after a card game?"

She creased her forehead. "You want to, don't you?"

"Of course I want to."

"So go ahead." Deliberately, she gave him her wicked smile that she'd practiced.

"You haven't answered my question," he said. "Is it what you want?"

Her smile melted away.

"I—"

She stopped. She couldn't say it.

He waited. Time passed, measured by the sound of their breathing.

She couldn't. It was too raw. Too huge. Too new.

"You want me to make the decision for you, don't you?" he asked, deep and gentle.

She nodded.

Oz took her arm. The touch wasn't sexual, but it sent a jolt through her anyway. He guided her to his chair, and sat her down in it, and he knelt in front of her on the floor and took her hands in his.

"When I make love with you, I want us to be in it together. Not because I've been carried away by how beautiful and sexy you are. And not because you're pretending to be somebody."

He lifted one of her hands to his lips and kissed it. The touch of his lips on her flesh flooded her with longing.

"Let's make it special, Marianne," he said. "Because you are."

He stood and picked up his cords from the floor. He was still hugely aroused, she noticed as she watched him get dressed.

"You're very honorable," she said. Her lips were finally unstuck now that he had his clothes on.

"Believe me, I'm kicking myself for it," he said. He retrieved her tank top and her jeans and handed them to her. She took them wordlessly, and he leaned forward and brushed a kiss on her forehead. Another touch that made her ache.

"But we will have sex with each other, Marianne," he said, still leaning forward, his breath warming the skin of her face. "It's a matter of when, not if. When you're ready, I intend to be there. And the waiting is going to make it even better."

CHAPTER TEN

IS THIS thing really supposed to go that far up my butt?

Marianne frowned over her shoulder at her reflection in the dressing-room mirror. The red PVC outfit clung to every curve of her body like a second shiny skin.

She turned around and surveyed her reflection from the front. She didn't look *bad* in it. Granted, it wasn't an outfit you would really want to wear on a casual Sunday stroll in the park, but she didn't want it for strolling. She wanted it for looking hot and naughty. Devilish.

In the week since the strip Go Fish game, Oz had come into Warren's bar most nights. He'd nursed a single beer and talked with her.

He'd said, that night when they'd stripped down to their underwear, that he'd wait to have sex with her. And she supposed, in a way, his hanging around the bar was his waiting. But it didn't feel as if he were waiting for sex; they'd talked like friends. About Daisy's crisis over the wedding table centerpieces, and her other crisis with the bridesmaids. About the music on the jukebox. About small, everyday things they had in common: favorite movies, loving the smell of peeled oranges, teachers they'd hated. And then two days ago, he'd invited her to a Hallowe'en costume party at his friend Jack's cinema. Costume theme of the movies.

It was a real date. And, as usual with a real date, she'd spent several waking hours wondering what she should wear.

Thinking about her new image, she'd made a beeline for the first bright red outfit she'd seen at the costume shop. The *Bedazzled* devil suit. She squinted at her breasts, which the zippered top pushed up practically to her chin, and pulled at the PVC.

How did people breathe in this stuff?

She pouted at herself experimentally. Sophisticated? Sexy? Satanic?

Or somebody with a really, really painful shiny sunburn?

She wriggled out of the outfit and into her own clothes and went back out on the shop floor to find another costume. It was no use trying to be the epitome of a bad girl if all you could think about was whether your pants were going to cut you in half.

She browsed through the costumes for rent and shook her head. She might as well find something to wear that she would feel comfortable in, and not have to worry about.

How come it had been so easy to choose the right dress for the biggest day of Oz's sister's life, after knowing her for five minutes, and now choosing a simple movie-theme costume for herself was like torture?

She ticked off possibilities in her head as she looked at costumes. Marilyn Monroe would involve wearing a wig, and wigs were scratchy. Lara Croft and Catwoman had the same skintight-costume problem. And Cruella DeVil would require far too much makeup.

This was getting silly. She had to choose something. And why was she worrying about what to wear in the first place? The whole point of a Hallowe'en costume was to pretend you were somebody else for a day. She didn't need to choose something to fit her new "bad girl" image. Oz had made it clear he didn't believe in that image, anyway.

She closed her eyes and waved her hand over the costume rack. She'd wear whatever she picked blind, as long as it was comfortable and not shaped like a gorilla.

Her fingers landed on soft cotton. She opened her eyes to see she was holding a gingham dress.

Marianne smiled. That would do. She'd even get to wear some cool shoes.

She waited for Oz just inside the bar, watching for him through the glass door. He'd said he'd come to her apartment, but her apartment was dingy and she'd just as soon he didn't see it again. She'd offered to meet him at the cinema, but Oz had insisted he'd escort her. Gentleman.

She'd adjusted the costume a little bit. Instead of wearing a blouse buttoned up to her neck underneath the blue gingham dress, she'd found a white top with a frill on the top that was quite a bit lower cut. It didn't show a lot of cleavage, but there was a little bit more than imagination there. She'd skipped the white bobby socks and worn sheer stockings to go with her ruby slippers. And though her hair was plaited into innocent braids, her mouth was outlined in red lipstick.

Okay, Dorothy was never going to be a bad girl. But she didn't have to be a nun.

She wondered what Oz would be wearing. Maybe his Hell's Angel outfit again. She closed her eyes and smiled as she pictured him in it.

The bar door opened. She opened her eyes and saw Oz: wearing jeans, a brown flannel shirt, a rope around his waist, and a floppy black hat. His blond hair stuck out from underneath it in an imitation of the straw that poked out from his wrists and ankles.

"You're the Scarecrow!" she said.

At the exact same time that he said, "You're Dorothy!" And they burst out laughing together.

"You're a very sexy Dorothy," he said, looking her up and down. She felt herself blush.

"It was just the first costume I came across. I didn't—" Suddenly she realized why Oz had dressed up as the Scarecrow. His name. Her cheeks felt even hotter.

"I didn't choose it because you're called—I mean, I closed my eyes. It was a random choice." She stopped, and looked up into his laughing, knowing hazel eyes. "You're going to say that nothing is random, aren't you?"

"It's a well-known theory that our subconscious expresses itself in our least deliberate actions," he replied, the laughter still in his voice.

Of course it did. She'd been thinking about Oz when she'd chosen the costume, blind choice or not.

She shrugged. "Whatever you say, Doc. Just don't get a big head." She walked past Oz out the door.

He caught up with her easily and took her arm. "I'm the Scarecrow, remember? Only straw in here." He tapped the side of his head. But she could tell from his smile that he was pleased.

Portland's downtown wasn't very big; the Delphi was just around the corner from Warren's bar, though she'd never been in it before. Oz pushed open the heavy wooden door for her, and they walked into a fantasy.

The theater was enormous, high-ceilinged, wood-paneled, elegant. And it was filled with every type of movie character, from cowboys to King Kong, laughing and holding drinks and dancing on the gleaming parquet floor.

A woman approached them. She was wearing the white belted dress and blaster of Princess Leia from the *Star Wars* films, but the buns of hair on either side of her head were vivid red instead of brown. "Oz!" she greeted him, standing on tiptoe to kiss him on the cheek, and then she'd turned to Marianne before she had a chance to get jealous, and shook her hand. "I'm Kitty Taylor. You must be Marianne. My husband, Jack, told me all about you."

"Nice to meet you," Marianne replied. "I think I was a little outspoken to your husband the last time I saw him."

"He probably deserved it," Kitty said cheerfully. "I have to put him in his place at least once a day. I'm glad you could come to our party."

Marianne took another look around the room. "This place is beautiful," she said. "It's exactly like stepping back in time."

"About eighty years, to be exact. The Delphi was built in nineteen twenty-six as a music hall," Jack said, joining them. He was dressed in a white shirt, black vest, and trousers with a stripe down the side. A blaster matching Kitty's hung from his low-slung belt. Han Solo to her Princess Leia. "Kitty and I finished the restorations last year. I'd be happy to tell you about the Delphi's history if you're interest—"

"Let the woman get a drink first," Kitty interrupted,

laughing. "He can talk about this place for hours," she told Marianne.

"And don't even get him started on the movies," Oz added.

Jack made a mock exasperated sound and turned to Oz. "What the hell are you wearing? The Scarecrow didn't have a brain. You've already got a brain. That's what gets you into trouble all the time."

"Ever hear of irony?"

Jack laughed. "Touché. Marianne, you make a great Dorothy."

"That accent's not from Kansas, though," Kitty said, walking with Marianne toward the tiled refreshment kiosk, the men following.

"No, South Carolina," Marianne answered.

"Really? It's a beautiful accent. Where in South Carolina? I was in a design firm in California with a woman from Charleston."

Kitty seemed very nice; Marianne liked her good-humored sparring with Jack, and the warmth in her green eyes. But no way was Marianne going to discuss Webb with her. "I'm from south of there. Did you grow up in Maine?"

Kitty looked at her for just a moment before answering, and Marianne knew she'd noticed her vagueness and change of the subject. But Kitty didn't say anything, instead keeping up a lively chatter about how she'd left Portland to live in California.

"And then I came back home to start my own business." Kitty handed Marianne a glass of punch. "I thought it was going to be easy. But everywhere I went in Portland, I saw reminders of my past. It's hard to make a whole new start. But worth it."

She raised her glass to Marianne's, and as they touched the brims together Marianne thought that Oz's friends were pretty clever people themselves. Kitty knew Marianne didn't want to talk about her past, and she was saying, without stating anything outright, that she respected Marianne's need to become someone new.

"Let's hope so," Marianne said, and drank.

"Cuz!" Warren came up to them. His dark hair was parted on the side and slicked back, and he wore a tight white T-shirt that clung to his lean body. Brando in *Streetcar.* He was accompanied by a woman in a bright green Peter Pan costume. "Hi, Kitty. Marianne, I'd like you to meet Lizzie, the director of the Inner Portland Youth Center. I think you might remember her from the other night."

Lizzie flung her arms around Marianne and hugged her. "You are just the most generous person I have ever met. Thank you, thank you, thank you so much for your donation. We never expected to make so much money, and boy do we need it right now."

"You—you're welcome," Marianne said, surprised by the woman's enthusiasm. And made a little sheepish by it. She'd only been thinking of Oz when she'd made her bid, not the youth center. "I'm afraid my motivations were completely selfish."

Lizzie glanced over at Oz, who was behind the counter of the refreshment kiosk with Jack, filling up the old-fashioned-looking popcorn machine. "And who can blame you?" she said, conspiratorially. "Oz Strummer is a catch. And he's helped us a lot with some of the disturbed kids at the center. I had him in my class when I was an elementary school teacher. Skinny little kid, and so serious all the time. He knew all the answers before I'd asked the questions. And this one—" she reached over and tweaked one of Kitty's Princess Leia buns "—was in the year below. Shy as a little sparrow, even with that bright red hair."

Kitty giggled. "See what I mean, Marianne? Everywhere I go, a reminder of my past."

"Lizzie was telling me that even though they raised more money at the bachelor auction than they thought they would, the center is still struggling," Warren said. "They could really use a volunteer who would help them with their fundraising and managing their expenditures. Someone with a background in marketing and business, maybe."

Warren stared hard at her as he said it.

"That's exactly what we need," Lizzie said. "My background is in working with kids, I'm just no good at the business side. But we can't afford to pay anybody, so the business types aren't interested."

"What do you think, Marianne?" Warren asked.

Marianne knew exactly what to think. Warren knew about her MBA and her executive marketing job at Webb Enterprises. He'd promised he'd keep her past a secret, but he darn well wanted her to let those particular facts out of the bag.

And she could help the youth center, if she decided to. She'd been good at her job in Webb. She'd probably be even better at promoting a worthy cause. It would feel good to use her training and experience to do something more valuable than to make a pile of money for a corporation.

But if she volunteered, she'd have to come clean about who she used to be.

"Why don't you contact some local businesses?" she suggested to Lizzie. "Or I bet the local Rotary club could help you find business-savvy people who are civic-minded enough to volunteer their time."

"That's an idea," Lizzie agreed. Marianne avoided Warren's eyes. Instead, she looked at Oz, who was carrying some boxes of popcorn toward them.

"Hi, Lizzie, Warren." Oz handed one of the boxes to Kitty. "Would you like popcorn, Marianne, or would you like to dance?"

"Dance," she said firmly. She wanted to get away from Warren and Lizzie and how selfish she felt. Plus, dancing with Oz would involve touching him.

"That's the answer I was hoping for," said Oz, and gave the other box of popcorn to Lizzie.

On the dance floor Oz put one hand on her waist and held her other in his. His fingers reached right round to the small of her back. He smelled of shampoo and flannel and the clean dry scent of straw. She laid her hand on his shoulder and they began to move together to the music.

She was selfish, and she was a coward, and she was repaying the kindness of these people she was meeting in Maine by not trusting them with her past.

"Oz," she said, "why do you like me? I mean, besides the sex thing."

"You mean the sex we haven't had yet?" He sounded amused, and when she looked up at his face his eyes were crinkled at the corners.

"I mean besides our being attracted to each other. I haven't told you anything about myself. You don't even know who I am. What makes you think you like me?"

"I don't think I like you. I know I like you."

"Why?"

He tilted his head and looked down at her. "At first, I thought it was because you were an intellectual challenge. You seem to have so many contradictions. I wanted to figure out what made you tick."

"And have you figured that out?"

And if he had, could he maybe fill her in?

"Not quite. But it's not the challenge I'm most attracted to anymore. It's you. I like your sense of humor and your vulnerability and your toughness and your wit. I like how you get angry with me and ask me unexpected questions."

"Like that one."

"Like that one." Oz smiled at her and twirled her around to the music. "And I like how you've obviously been trained to be light as a feather when you dance."

Her daddy had taught her how to dance. She'd followed his lead on the dance floor, as she'd followed it all her life. Until she'd left Webb.

"People think we put on costumes to disguise who we really are," Oz said. "But I'm beginning to understand that it's when we pretend to be other people that we reveal the most about ourselves." He spun her around again, and then settled her more firmly in his arms. "For example, I felt silly in that motorcycle outfit when I first put it on. But as soon as I met you and saw how you saw me in it, I realized that I'd been denying my reckless side for far too long."

"You're not brainless like the Scarecrow, though."

"No. I'm the opposite. I've always defined myself by my intellect. I thought that was one thing that made me different. At the end of the film, the Scarecrow realizes that he's had brains all along. I've been a nerd all my life, Marianne. I don't look much like one now, but I'm still a nerd inside. I'm starting to see that there's more to me than brains."

"There's definitely more. I think you've got a bigger heart than the Tin Man ever did."

"And like Dorothy, you've come a very long way to find out whether there's no place like home."

She blinked at him. "I really just chose this costume by mistake," she said.

"No, you didn't," Oz said. "And you haven't chosen any of your other disguises by mistake, either." He gently pulled her tighter to him. "I'm hoping that one day you'll trust me with your past. But until then, I'm enjoying learning about you through your masks."

Oz spent the rest of the evening dancing with her and introducing her to his friends and joking with her and Jack and Kitty. At midnight, they all went into the cinema to watch a screening of *Halloween*. The screen room had gilded walls, and silver stars on the double-height ceiling, and lush red velvet seats. Oz sat with his arm around Marianne's shoulder and squeezed her every time she jumped at the murderer's appearance.

After the movie, they said goodbye to everyone—except Warren, who was deep in intense conversation with a good-looking man dressed like John Travolta in *Grease*—and left the Delphi hand in hand.

The weather had turned cold outside. Marianne shivered in her thin frock, and Oz drew her to his side.

"If you clicked your ruby slippers together, you could get us home right away and you wouldn't be cold," he said.

"There's no place like home," she said, and clicked her heels together. The evening had been so magical, she wouldn't have been surprised if a tornado had picked them up.

No place like home.

She wondered what "home" meant, after all. Webb? Or someplace where people accepted her without knowing her background or reputation? As they had tonight?

"You hungry?" Oz asked as they passed a late-night diner. The light from the windows spilled out onto the street, along with the smell of french fries and meat on the grill. Her stomach growled.

"Definitely," she said. They went in and got a booth near a window and ordered cheeseburgers and fries. They pooled their quarters and fed them into the fifties-style jukebox selector mounted near their table, arguing good-naturedly about which songs to play. Oz tried to find a song called "Marianne" but had to settle for "Mary's Prayer" by Danny Wilson. In revenge, she played "Goodbye Yellow Brick Road" by Elton John.

As she bit into her cheeseburger Marianne was reminded forcibly of how much things had changed for her. Not so long ago, she never could have ordered something so casually indulgent, so normal as a cheeseburger and fries. Let alone eaten it. In public, in front of a window. Using her fingers to dip the fries in ketchup, licking melted cheese off her wrist when it dribbled out of the bun. It would have been an unthinkable weakness.

She watched Oz eating. His sculpted mouth and even white teeth biting into his burger. His perfect, golden-skinned throat swallowing. The way his lips kissed the rim of his glass of milk.

She'd come a long way, but she wasn't home yet.

If she were, she would be able to express her hunger for Oz in the same easy way she could pop a fry into her mouth. She'd be able to talk about her past with as much confidence as she'd had giving her order to the diner's waitress.

"I've had a really good time tonight," Oz said, pushing his empty plate away.

"Me too," she said, surprised to find that her plate was as empty as his.

"I still owe you a real date," he said. "A dress-up-and-go-out-to-dinner date. The sort of thing you paid three thousand dollars for."

The mention of three thousand dollars reminded her of the fact that she hadn't been able to overcome her past enough to volunteer her time to Lizzie.

"I'm fine with the party, the movies, and the cheeseburger," she said. "Donate the money you would've spent to the youth center instead."

"I'll do both," Oz said, and covered his mouth with his hand as he yawned. "You're not boring," he said; "I was up early this morning going over case notes."

"A hard day analyzing patients, and a hard night analyzing costumes," she said lightly. "Kitty wasn't joking tonight when she told me you worked too much."

"I work too much," he agreed, standing up and putting a bill on the table for their food. "But they're my responsibilities. I'm not going to run away from them."

It was even colder outside than it had been before they'd gone into the diner. As they walked the half a block back to Warren's bar and her apartment Marianne mused over Oz's choice of words. Usually when he said something with a double meaning, he looked her straight in the eye, his head tilted in that thoughtful way. He hadn't been doing that when he'd talked about his responsibilities. He'd been talking purely about himself.

But his words had hit home anyway. She'd run away from all of her responsibilities: her family, her job, her place in Webb. And she didn't have enough guts to take on any new responsibilities here in Portland.

For the second time, she wished fervently that Oz had been the man he'd appeared to be the first time she'd seen him. Not just because she'd wanted to be a bad girl having a wild fling with a bad man, but because everything good about Oz made her see all too clearly just how inadequate she was.

Oz walked her down the alleyway to the parking lot and the door to her apartment. "Thank you for a wonderful time," he said, his arm still around her.

"Thank you, too," she said. She had a strong urge to press herself against his chest, feel him holding her, smoothing down her hair and comforting her. As he'd done with his sister when she'd cried about her wedding dress.

"I want to kiss you goodnight," he said, "but if I do, it won't be goodnight."

She nodded. And stood on tiptoe and kissed him on the side of his jaw, just below the bone, where his pulse beat. She breathed in a lungful of his scent.

"Goodnight," she whispered, and then she turned and ran up the stairs to her apartment, her ruby slippers flashing in the dim light.

CHAPTER ELEVEN

THE ice in the aluminum container made a funky sound like maracas as she shook it. Marianne deftly replaced the cap with a strainer and poured the liquid into a hurricane glass filled with ice. Without looking, she grabbed the jug of orange juice from below the bar and filled the glass nearly to the rim. Then, carefully, she held the bottle of 151-proof rum over it, floating a layer of the dark liquor on the top of the drink. A cherry and some pineapple on a cocktail stick, a little bamboo umbrella, and she pushed the drink over to Warren.

He took a sip and closed his eyes in pleasure. "A perfect Zombie, in under a minute. Cuz, you've turned into a master mixologist."

She gestured at the battered cocktail recipe book, and shrugged. "A to Z in three weeks. All it takes is practice."

Warren leaned his elbows on the polished bar. Mid-afternoon on a Sunday, the place wasn't busy, and he'd been hanging a new string of chili lights around the booths in the corner. "It's more than practice. It's dedication. You've always been able to do anything you decided to." He took another tiny sip of the Zombie, and pushed it to her. "I can't drink this at two p.m. Don't you want to taste your own creation?"

"No, thanks. I don't really like alcohol." She dumped the drink down the sink, rinsed off the cherry and the pineapple slice, and ate them.

Warren laughed. "You're even good at things you don't like. I should have savored those few days when you couldn't pour beer. I think that was the last time in my life I'll ever be better at something than you are."

Her cousin's voice had been light, but Marianne looked at him sharply anyway. "Warren, are my ears going funny? You almost sounded jealous."

"Honey, I've always been jealous of you. Pour me a ginger ale, will you?"

Cheerful, carefree Warren. Her cousin who'd been allowed to play, who had a nice, soft, homey mother and a bedroom full of the most interesting junk.

"You're so much cooler than I am," she said, filling a glass for him. "You've always done just what you wanted and not had to worry about anything."

"Oh, sweetheart," he said, shaking his head, "I worried about plenty, believe me. You try growing up gay in Webb. Especially with our last name."

"Your mother didn't mind you being gay, though." Marianne had always loved Aunt Judy; even, in her most secret, traitorous thoughts, wishing her own mother had been more like her. Uncle Graham, her father's younger brother, had died fairly young, and Judy and Warren were far more relaxed than her own family.

"My mother didn't mind. No."

There was some emphasis in that sentence that she didn't understand. Warren had always just been—

Warren. He hadn't had anything to live up to. She'd thought he'd been happy to be himself.

"But you wanted to leave, didn't you?" she asked. "You wanted to go to New York, where everything was wilder and more exciting?"

"I didn't have much choice. I—" Warren hesitated, and then took a sip of his ginger ale and smiled at her. "Anyway, I was never like you, Marianne. You just belonged in Webb. It was as if the world was made for you. I was so shocked when you came up here and wanted to forget all about it."

She winced. "I'm sorry about Lizzie, Warren. I really do want to help her. But I'm—it's too soon to let people know what I've come from."

He nodded. "Okay, hon, your choice. Maybe you'll rethink that later. I don't think people will judge you, you know. It's pretty clear that you're as popular here as you used to be in Webb."

"That's such a weird way of looking at it," she said, "because I never fit in in Webb. I was always the special one, I was always different from everybody else. And since I've been here, I've had to work and work to fit in, too."

That was what it had been, she realized. Work. Trying so hard to be what she'd decided to be.

It had been an emotional roller coaster since she'd come to Portland. She'd had some scared moments, and some tearful moments. Angry moments. And moments of exhilaration—climbing on the bar and bidding all the money she had. Watching Oz's face as she peeled off her jeans.

Those moments had made her feel more alive than she'd ever felt.

But the times she'd been truly happy were times like this, when she didn't have to play any games. Like right now, talking with Warren. And when she'd been with Oz: on the back of the Harley, carried in his arms through bright leaves, learning about his family. Dancing last night at the party, smiling across at him in the diner.

Every time Oz laughed, or looked at her so closely with his hazel eyes, she felt somehow real.

Warren was nodding at her. "I can see, now, that it was hard for you in Webb. At the time, though, I thought you had it all." He drained his ginger ale and swirled the ice around in his glass. "Anyway. In the end, I'm glad I didn't fit in. It made me find out who I was and what I wanted. I thought I wanted the high life in New York, but then I decided I liked the quiet, business-owning life in Maine."

The bar door opened, and Warren turned on his stool to see who'd come in. It was a slim guy with fashionably spiky hair, carrying several shopping bags. He spotted Warren and waved. Marianne recognized him as the man who'd been dressed up as John Travolta last night. Her cousin beamed and hopped off the stool.

"Relatively quiet life," he amended, giving Marianne one of his winks, and went to greet his friend.

Marianne rinsed out the Zombie glass and put it in the glass washer. She watched Warren and his friend spread out his purchases on one of the tables: a garden gnome, a framed poster of a fifties lingerie ad, some sort of feathery thing. Obviously more eclectic decor for the bar. Warren, chatting and giving his friend little flirtatious touches, looked happy. As he'd said he was.

He'd traveled to Maine and found himself.

And she'd traveled to Maine and found…who?

Not a born-again bad girl. Oz was right: that was a role, and it was something she had to work at. She liked parts of it. The power, for example. The forthrightness she could summon when she was playing a role.

But it wasn't her.

She dried her hands on a dish towel and went up to her apartment, leaving Warren and his friend to hold down the fort. It was her day off, actually. She'd only been downstairs to make that last cocktail in the book, and to chat with Warren. And because she didn't have much else to do.

Once she'd got the hang of making drinks, tending bar wasn't really a challenge. It was sort of fun, quite relaxing at times, she liked meeting the people, but it wasn't exactly absorbing.

She climbed the dusty stairs to her apartment and let herself in.

Marianne bet that Oz could look at a person's home and guess things about their psychology just from the state of their kitchen table. She stood in the doorway and surveyed the apartment she'd lived in for the past three weeks and tried to see what it said about her personality.

The linoleum was cracked, and scattered here and there with mismatched rag rugs. One of the cupboard doors in the kitchenette hung from one hinge. The curtains looked as if they'd come from a nineteen-seventies yard sale and the fridge and the oven were in a desperately ugly shade of avocado.

As she watched, a brown spider the size of a quarter scuttled across the floor and underneath the spindly wooden chair that was the only place to sit down. She could've sworn it was the same spider she'd trapped and thrown out the window this morning. Then again, from the cobwebs that always appeared overnight, there was a spider family of Brady Bunch dimensions sharing her apartment with her.

According to her apartment, she had the personality of a battered seventies throwback arachnophile.

"Enough is enough," she said, hearing her voice loud in her ears in the tiny apartment.

She didn't like living in squalor. It might be fine for a so-called bad girl, but it wasn't fine for her. She wanted to have a comfortable sofa where she could sit and talk with her friends and she wanted to have a bed that didn't sink down in the middle. She didn't want to have to scoop spiders out of the shower every morning. In fact, she didn't even want a shower. She wanted a bath.

She wanted a long, hot bath, and she wanted to spend her afternoon off with someone that she liked. Relaxing and having fun, and not having to live up to any image.

She closed the door behind her and went to her refrigerator. A business card was stuck onto its avocado surface with a lobster-shaped magnet. She pulled it off and looked at the phone number written on the back. Oz's handwriting was firm, well formed, and clear. It reflected his personality in a way that her apartment didn't reflect hers.

Marianne picked up the phone.

It was official. He had lost his mind.

Oz stood in his cold driveway, his breath coming in clouds, his hands shoved into the pockets of his jeans, looking at the Harley.

Which was now *his* Harley.

His Harley that gleamed bright red and chrome, that looked like freedom on two wheels, and that had cost him a substantial chunk of his savings and an even more considerable proportion of his dignity.

He'd had to beg Kitty's brother, Nick Giroux, to sell it to him. As Kitty had said, it was Nick's pride and joy. Oz had had to resort to wheedling Kitty into taking his side and persuading her brother that with the money he got from selling Oz the motorcycle, he could buy another one and fix it up from scratch.

Oz's behavior was obsessive, it was manipulative, it was extravagant, and it had been completely irresistible.

In other words: he was so far gone that he had bought a motorcycle just because it made him feel the smallest fraction as wonderful as Marianne did when he was with her.

He'd been too damn responsible to have sex with her when she'd clearly wanted to, just because it hadn't seemed like the right time and place, and because he'd wanted her heart to be in it. So in some kind of crazy opposite reaction, he'd bought a Harley.

He'd bought a *Harley.* What was he thinking?

He pulled in a deep breath to sigh, and smelled a slightly metallic edge to the chill air. To someone born and brought up in Maine, that smell meant snow, even on the first day of November.

"This motorcycle is going to be as useless as a roller skate in the snow," he muttered to himself.

He had patients. He had two jobs. He had responsibilities. And he'd spent a lot of evenings in a bar, and spent a lot of money on a motorcycle he wouldn't even be able to ride for the next five months

To say nothing of the fact that he'd been outside to gaze at this Harley Davidson three times in the past hour, when he should have been working on his lecture notes. And the fact that every single time he looked at the Harley, he thought of Marianne. Riding it. Wrapped around him. In the bar, naked except for two wisps of maddening red lace. Blushing and smiling and seductive.

Oz sighed again and opened his garage door and wheeled the Harley inside next to his Honda where it wouldn't be touched by the snow, when it came.

He couldn't resist a last look at it before he closed the garage door and went back into the house. It was a beautiful machine. A beautiful, fast, loud, useless machine that he owned purely for his own pleasure.

He didn't bother to suppress his grin.

But when he opened his refrigerator to get out a bottle of water, he saw once again the six-pack of diet soda that his sister Daisy had left behind, and, at last, he hoicked it out and put it on the counter by the sink. He'd bring it in to his receptionist tomorrow.

The soda symbolized his need to have someone intimate in his life, someone he loved unconditionally, as he did his family. Keeping it was irrational and it wasn't helping him concentrate. The motorcycle was bad enough.

His phone rang. Probably Jack calling to tease him about his Harley purchase. When Jack had spent a huge amount of money buying the then-derelict Delphi theater, Oz had taken great enjoyment in suggesting that Jack had purchased the vast erection because he hadn't had sex in nearly a year.

Oz swung his fridge door shut with his foot while reaching for the receiver.

"I'm not having an early midlife crisis, and I don't

want to hear anything about not getting laid, either," he said, without any preamble. "I just wanted it, okay?"

There was a pause.

"That's fine; I like a man who knows what he wants."

Her voice, sweet as cold tea on a hot day.

"Marianne," he said, squeezing his eyes shut and dropping his forehead into his hand. "How are you?"

"I'm just dandy, though you sound a little preoccupied, if you don't mind me saying. Do you have a bathtub?"

"Yes." *What?*

"Do you mind if I use it?"

"Um." Oz got a full-senses mental picture of Marianne, naked, in his bathtub, her perfect skin flushed pink with heat, her hair in damp tendrils around her face, the room full of her scent. The sudsy water lapping the tops of her breasts. Her graceful feet with their cherry-red nails propped on the end of the bath, exposing her delicate ankles and curvy calves. In his imagination, he watched a drop of water trickle from the arch of her throat, over her collarbone, and disappear down the valley of her cleavage.

He swallowed.

"You want to take a bath?" he asked.

"That was the idea. I haven't had a bath in ages and I could do with some relaxation. Do you mind?"

He could think of nothing in the universe he would like more than Marianne Webb in his bathtub.

She said she wanted to relax, he told himself. *Not have hot sex with you in the bathtub.*

Then again, hot sex was one of the best relaxation aids in the world.

"Of course I don't mind," he said, trying to keep his voice friendly and laid-back. "Come on over."

"How do I get to your house?"

He gave her directions, all the time thinking frantically. Was this another one of her seduction ideas? A way to make him lose control?

"I'll be there in about half an hour," Marianne was saying. "I'll bring my own bubble bath, but I might have to borrow a towel."

Oz gripped the phone receiver so hard he thought it might crack any minute. "All right, see you soon," he said, and put the phone down, and sank into a kitchen chair.

He'd promised himself, and Marianne, that he would not have sex with her until she was ready—and until she told him she was ready. There was something haunting her, something probably from her past that she couldn't let go, and he didn't want their time together, whatever it led to, to be tainted by even the tiniest bit of doubt.

That meant that Marianne would have her bath alone.

He had an unnecessary Harley Davidson in his garage and in half an hour the most desirable woman he'd ever met was going to be naked in his house and he wasn't going to allow himself to have sex with her.

Oz pressed his forehead to the cool surface of his table.

If he wasn't clinically insane already, he was going to be, very very soon.

Now this was exactly what the doctor had ordered.

Marianne stretched out her foot, turned on the faucet with her toes, and let a stream of blissfully hot water flow into the slowly cooling bath. The entire bathroom was full of steam and the scent of the floral bubbles she'd bought on her way over to Oz's house. Her fingers and her toes were white and pruney, and her whole body felt soothed and calm.

She wondered what the doctor was actually doing right now.

She'd been surprised to see that Oz's house was rambling, old, Victorian, with white-painted clapboards. He'd greeted her at the door and brought her straight up the rather grand wooden staircase to the bathroom. The *guest* bathroom, he'd said. With a certain emphasis on "guest", which had fit well with his demeanor, which was as courteous and laid-back as always, and yet a little distant.

But his voice and his hands had betrayed him. She was wearing jeans and a sweater, nothing sexy, but she could recognize when a man was devouring her with his eyes. As she'd been devouring him. She hadn't come here to seduce him, but she couldn't help looking. When their eyes had met, as he'd opened the bathroom door for her…

Marianne sighed and sank deeper into the bath's embrace. That one look had been sizzling, and she'd been able to read his thoughts as if he'd spoken them aloud. *This is the room where you're going to get naked and I really want to join you.*

When she'd glanced down, she'd seen his hand white-knuckled on the doorknob, noticed how the tendons of his wrist had been tense, as if he'd been restraining himself.

"Enjoy your bath," he said, and his voice was tense, too. "I've got lecture notes to do, so I'll be downstairs in my study. If you need me, just yell."

He stepped back. "I mean, if you need anything."

"I know what you meant," she said, and the look he gave her before he turned away was almost agonized.

Despite the hot water, Marianne shivered. A lazy tendril of desire curled through her, making her limbs feel even more languorous, and her skin even more tingly.

Oz wanted her badly. He was trying not to act on it, but he couldn't hide it.

Was he really working downstairs? Or was he, like her, thinking about the attraction between them?

She smiled. A hot, frothy bath in a glorious claw-footed tub, fluffy towels waiting for her on the radiator, and Oz sitting downstairs probably picturing her naked and not doing anything about it because he respected her.

This was what she wanted: moments like this to savor. Something so cosy, so warm, so safe, and so exciting at the same time. She didn't have to live up to anything, or to please anybody else. She just had to enjoy this bath, and this big, white-tiled bathroom, and then go downstairs and see what Oz had on his mind.

She stretched once more, and then stood and stepped out of the bath, reaching for the towel. As she dried herself every stroke of the soft cotton on her skin made her think about Oz.

It was his towel. Had he used it on his naked, wet body? Rubbing it against his perfect chest, as she was doing with her breasts right now, the terrycloth an exquisite teasing on her nipples? Had he rubbed a path down his body, stroked it down his powerful thighs?

She propped her foot up on the side of the emptying bath and as she dried her legs she thought about running her hands down his legs. Taking the towel like this, and reaching between his thighs. Kneeling down in front of him and drying him carefully, slowly, letting her hands and the towel caress his hips and downward.

She'd dry every inch of him. Look at him as she knelt

in front of him. Feast her eyes and her hands. Listen to that soft turned-on growl in the back of his throat.

What would he taste like? Warm and clean from a bath?

The towel dropped to her own crotch and she sucked in a quick breath as her hand stroked against her over-excited flesh.

For a moment, she stood there and just enjoyed it, the towel and her hand pressed against herself. Like the bath, like the afternoon, like the man: pleasure for its own sweet sake.

She thought of what Oz would do if he walked in on her right now. She imagined him taking the towel gently from her hand and putting it on the floor, and then slipping his own fingers into the damp curls between her legs, where she felt so hot and heavy, wet and ready for him. She would tangle her hand in his hair and steady herself with the other one on his broad shoulder. And he would flick the tip of one finger against her clitoris, sensual and slow, and then slide his long finger deep, deep inside her—

Marianne's vision became a white blur and she felt her world convulse around her. The floor moved. The walls moved. The bath moved. Her body shuddered and she staggered back, her legs suddenly weak, gasping and blinking her eyes and leaning against the edge of the tub trying to collect herself.

Then she giggled. Her heart was pounding, her skin was flushed. Her body felt relaxed, and invigorated, and so darn alive.

She'd just given herself an orgasm, almost by mistake. Just...because.

Marianne grinned as she dressed herself and brushed her hair. She hung the towel carefully on the radiator and went downstairs to find Oz, her heart still pounding. Curious to know what she would do next. As she crossed the hallway, she hummed.

She felt *good.*

Oz's house was big, clean and uncluttered, just on the shabby side of comfortable. The walls were plain white and the floors were well-worn wood. She wandered into the living room. The overstuffed furniture was old, and the rug was threadbare in places. Nothing quite matched. The low coffee table had scratches on it. It looked as if it got used as a footstool, a dining table, and—she looked more closely at the scratches—a bottle opener. She pictured Oz sprawled on the couch reading a book late at night, a box of take-out pizza forgotten on the table. Probably reading five books at once, knowing him. The bookshelves lining the walls were full.

It wasn't squalor. It showed a disregard for style in favor of comfort that was very, very male. And very different from the polished, scratch-free house she'd grown up in.

She started humming again and went through a door into the kitchen, another big room with battered, comfortable furniture. Only two of the six chairs around the table matched, and there was a six-pack of diet cola on the counter. Not her brand, but Marianne was thirsty, so she pulled one off and snapped the tab open, and looked around the room again.

Her eyes widened.

Somehow, she'd been so mellow and happy and interested in Oz's house, she'd missed seeing what was going on outside the window.

It was pure white.

Flakes of snow sifted through the air, fast and soft,

like an exploded pillow. She ran to the window and looked out at Oz's backyard. It was blanketed with the snow that had fallen since she'd been in her bath. Clumps of it lined the trees.

"Oz!" she cried in delight, and didn't even pause to put down her can before she was out of the kitchen, in the hallway, looking through doorways to find his study.

It was right at the back of the house, past a dining room and another spacious room that held a rowing machine and some weights. The door was half open. Marianne pushed it open and paused for a second on the threshold, taking it in.

Books and papers. Stuffed with them. Scattered with them. Framed diplomas and photographs on the walls between the bookcases. An intellectual chaos. Oz sat in the middle of it, in a black leather chair, his elbows propped up on a desk surrounded by stacks of paper, his hands buried in hair almost as chaotic as the room. He had a pen behind his ear.

"Oz!" she said again.

He took his hands out of his hair and looked at her. Her hot cheeks, her damp hair, her eyes that she knew were shining, the can of diet cola in her hand.

"You're the perfect woman, did you know that?" he asked, and his voice was dazed.

"It's snowing!" she said, almost bursting with the excitement of it.

"I know," he said, shaking his head, "and it's the first day of November. That's early even for Maine."

She waded through the towers of books and papers on the floor and grabbed his arm. "Come on, Oz, we've got to go outside in it." She pulled at him.

He was so much bigger than her that it was like

pulling on a wall, but he got up and followed along with her as she tugged him out of his study. "Haven't you seen snow before?"

"Of course I've seen snow before. Just not so much of it so fast. Come on."

"You're a bossy little thing, aren't you?" he said, but he was smiling. They reached the front door and pushed on their shoes. "Hold on." He opened a closet in the wall and pulled out his leather jacket and a winter coat, which he handed to her. "I'm not sure if they teach you this in South Podunk, but snow is cold. Gloves are in the pocket."

The coat came down to her knees. She pulled on the gloves but was too impatient to zip up the coat. "Come on, come on, it'll disappear," she urged. Her hands swam in the gloves, and the doorknob kept slipping out of her grasp.

"Don't worry, it's plenty cold enough to stick," he said, and opened the door for her. She was out of it like a shot, flying down the front stairs into a world of sparkling crystal feathers.

"Oh," she said, stopping still and turning around. There had to be six inches of it on the ground already. It covered her sneakers and made a muffled squeaking sound when she moved. Everything looked different, soft and rounded, grass smoothed over, road a pristine ribbon, her car a contoured lump.

And the snow had a scent, icy and silver. And a sound, a soft, cottony murmur as it settled on the ground around her and on her face with cold kisses. It was falling so fast she almost felt as if she were moving upward toward the sky.

She felt Oz next to her as a big, warm presence. "Do you like it?" he asked.

"It's sparklier than in South Carolina," she said. "Like lots of crystals. And it smells different."

"It's colder," he said. He surveyed the rapidly accumulating drifts. "It's quite a storm."

They'd only been outside for seconds, but already he had flakes in his eyelashes and clinging to his blond hair.

"Let's walk in it." She linked her arm through his and they headed down the silent street. She looked back and saw their footprints, one set of small ones, one set of large ones, side by side.

"Can we make a big snowman?" she asked, but Oz shook his head.

"Too cold. The snow won't stick together. I think you could make a snowball, though, if you used your bare hands." He bent and scooped up a handful of snow, packing it into a ball with his long fingers.

At nearly the last moment she realized that the only person around to throw a snowball at was her. She squealed and snatched her arm out of his, and ran ahead down the road, pulling her gloves off with her teeth and snagging her own handful of snow for retaliation.

His snowball hit her in the shoulder. She whirled around and threw hers. It disintegrated before it had gone three feet.

"You call that a snowball?" Oz taunted, and she saw him picking up another handful. Fast, laughing, her breath coming in clouds, she formed another snowball, pressing it hard this time, and whizzed it at him sidearm.

It got him in the side of the head. He clapped his hand to the spot, looking stunned.

"I learn fast, Dr. Strummer!" she called.

"Right," she heard him mutter. "This is the Civil War all over again." He launched himself forward.

She turned and ran, but her sneakers slipped in the snow. She scrambled to her feet, laughing and panting, running even before she'd gotten up, but it was too late. Oz seized her around the waist and swung her around to face him.

"Let go, you big lug!" She giggled, and slid her feet around, trying to get purchase on the snow. Her toe caught something, the curb maybe, and she pushed against him.

Oz's feet went out from underneath him. He landed with a thud in a drift of snow on his back, and Marianne tumbled after him, sprawled on top of him.

The impact against his hard chest knocked the breath out of her for a second. Then she looked up into his face and her breath was stolen away for real.

Oz, surrounded by diamonds. His face perfect, his smile as dazzling as the snow, and his eyes hazel spring. His breath in a cloud, as if it were too precious to disappear. As she watched a snowflake landed on his lower lip and she saw its complex, geometric form melt into a drop of pure water.

He was warm and unmoving underneath her, the only fixed point in a world of swirling white and cold.

"Marianne," he said, low and deep in his throat.

"You said our first time together should be special," she said.

"Yes."

"I think," she said, and her own voice was a whisper, "I think it's special now."

She saw him bite his lip, and let it go.

"It's always been special," he said.

She pressed her mouth to his. Slowly, deliberately. Exactly as she wanted to.

His lips were cold. Hers were, too. She let the kiss linger until they were warmed.

And then she looked into his eyes.

"I want you," she said, loud and clear.

CHAPTER TWELVE

THE minute she said it, Marianne felt the same exhilaration come rushing back, the same joyous recklessness and power. Only this time she wasn't pretending to be anybody else.

"Oz, I want you," she said again.

He'd been searching her eyes, his face serious, but now his smile came back again.

"Good," he said. "Do you want me inside the house, or right here?"

"Inside," she answered, wriggling a little bit on him, feeling even more wonderful with the double entendre.

"Good," he said again. "I think I could probably perform here, but I'd risk frostbite to my buttocks."

He sat up, adjusting her in his arms, and then knelt and stood, holding her aloft, cradled to his chest.

"And that would be a horrible waste of a perfect backside," Marianne agreed as she wrapped her arms around his neck.

"You should probably reserve judgement about the perfection of my backside until you actually see it."

Marianne nuzzled the side of his neck, where his jacket was open. "Get me inside, then," she murmured, and just touched his skin with the tip of her tongue.

He ran. Surefooted and crunching through the snow, up the road and up the front steps of his house and through the door. He kicked it shut behind him and stood in the hallway, cheeks flushed with the cold, holding her and looking into her eyes.

"You're sure?"

"I've never been more sure of anything," she said.

"Bedroom?"

"Now."

Oz's feet left clumps of snow and puddles across the wooden floor and up the wooden staircase. She couldn't wait to start touching him; she kissed his damp hair, his chilled face, his slightly rough-skinned jaw. She burrowed her hands underneath his jacket and his flannel shirt to grip the bare skin of his shoulders.

"I want to take your clothes off," she whispered into his ear as they reached his bedroom, and she heard a strangled sound in his throat. Then he'd placed her on her feet and he was kissing her hungrily.

She tore at his clothes, kissing him all the time. Pushed his jacket off and onto the floor. She worked her way down the buttons of his shirt by feel and then she pulled her mouth away from his and kissed his bare chest as it was exposed to her, inch by inch. He had crisp blond hair and sculpted muscles. She felt him trying to pull off her coat—his coat, that she was wearing—so she shrugged it off and kept on paying attention to his chest.

Magnificent. Even better than it had been the other night, because now she could touch him. She put her lips to one of his small male nipples and sucked on him, as she remembered him doing to her, that night they had met, and was rewarded by the hardening of his flesh, and the sound and feel of him groaning.

A pause as he tugged her sweater over her head, and then she was exploring his chest some more with her hands and mouth. His stomach muscles were like iron under her lips, moving in and out with his fast breathing. His ribs covered by smooth, golden skin.

"Marianne," she heard him say, and he pulled her up by the shoulders to kiss her mouth again. Even more frantic and desperate than it had been a moment ago. His lips weren't cold anymore; they were hot, searing. He nearly tore off her T-shirt, only stopping kissing her for a split second. Her impatient fingers fumbled with his belt buckle.

"Help me," she said into his mouth. And somehow, in a kind of complicated, awkward dance, their kiss never ending, Oz kicked off his shoes and helped her unfasten his belt and his jeans, and then pull them down his legs. They tangled around his ankles and he stumbled back from her, laughing, breaking their kiss.

Her own jeans were wet and would be a nightmare to get off. She sat on the edge of his bed and toed off her sneakers and then wriggled her jeans down. She watched him the whole time she was undressing. He was wearing green and white checked boxer shorts, and his erection strained against them.

Marianne's mouth began to water. She ripped her jeans and socks off and tossed them onto the floor, and stood up.

"Here we are again in our underwear," she said. Her heart was pounding so hard she could hear it. She suspected Oz could probably see it, above the soft pink cup of her bra.

Oz was shaking his head, his eyes traveling over her, his mouth slightly open.

"You are absolutely gorgeous," he said. "I can't believe I'm lucky enough to have you in my bedroom."

"I used to be a beauty queen," she said, and then realized that that was the first thing she'd ever deliberately told him about her past.

"I'm not surprised. But you're not just beauty-queen gorgeous. You're *you* gorgeous."

He stepped forward and touched one finger to the strap of her pink cotton bra, then trailed it down the side of her breast, down the curve of her waist to her hip, to the top of her pink cotton panties. Her underwear was plain and comfortable, not particularly revealing. Pretty much the polar opposite of her flaming-red bad-girl lingerie.

And Marianne knew she was the sexiest she'd ever been.

"I want to watch you take off your underwear," she told him.

He nodded, and he was still smiling. She could feel herself smiling.

They were getting naked, she was ordering him around, and they were grinning like a couple of fools.

But when he took off his underwear she felt her smile disappear.

He was…stunning. Godlike.

There was a V of muscle from the top of his hips, toward his groin, she didn't even know what to call it except for amazing. And his erection jutted outward and upward toward her.

She'd thought she could imagine what it was like from seeing it through his briefs the other night. No chance. She couldn't have imagined something that erotic even if she'd been practicing at being a bad girl for twenty years.

She remembered the fantasy she'd had in the bathroom earlier, and she licked her lips.

"What do you want, Marianne?" Oz asked her, his voice serious. "Tell me."

"I want."

Her voice failed her. This wasn't just *wanting*. This was wanting. And saying it out loud.

She took a deep breath, and squared her shoulders, and tried again.

"I want to touch you," she said. "I want to taste you. I want you in my mouth."

It was Oz's turn not to be able to speak.

He shut his mouth. He widened his eyes. He opened his mouth again, and then closed it, and then opened it and his breath came out in a whoosh.

Oz nodded.

Marianne stepped toward him. She held out her hand, palm up. She could feel the heat from his arousal even before she touched him. Then he was in her hand, branding her palm, alive and virile, and she closed her fingers around his girth.

She weighed him in her hand. Explored his length, the smooth, elastic skin. Watching his face as she did. She'd have time to look at where she was touching in a minute. Right now, she wanted to see him reacting to her.

And he was. His pupils were dilated. His breath was coming in short pants.

She knelt down in front of him and touched the tip of him with the tip of her tongue.

He tasted wonderful. Everything she had fantasized

about and more. His skin was velvet and salty. With a soft sound of appreciation in her throat she opened her mouth and took him in.

He growled. She loved that sexy growl. She felt his hands settle on her head and take gentle handfuls of her hair.

She couldn't fit all of him in her mouth. But she made slow swirls of her tongue around the head of his penis, and sucked him as deep as she could. Once. Twice. Feeling powerful, and desired.

And then he was drawing her upward to stand on her feet. She felt his hardness, wet from her mouth, press against her naked belly as she stood.

"I can't take much more of that," he muttered roughly, pressing kisses on her forehead, her cheeks, her lips. "How do you know what's going to drive me wild?"

"I used to be a good girl," she said, licking her lips, still savoring his taste and the memory of how he felt.

"You're still very, very good." With firm hands on her shoulders he directed her backward, toward his bed. She scrambled onto it and pulled him down after her.

"I want to please you, Marianne," Oz said, wrapping his arm around her waist and pulling her to lie full-length against him. "Would you believe I had a fantasy about what you would sound like having an orgasm within ten minutes of meeting you?"

"Really?"

"Uh-huh." He traced her hip with his hand. "Can't wait to find out if I was right."

"I had a fantasy this afternoon," she said, before she could hesitate. "In your bathroom."

He was running his hand up her front, over her bra,

stirring all sorts of wonderful sensations. "Hmm? About what?"

"You touching me. Making me come." She did have to whisper for this one. "I had an orgasm just from thinking about it."

He rolled her over on her back and lay over her, his body propped up on his muscular arms. "Have I mentioned lately that you are the perfect woman?"

"You haven't mentioned it for a little while."

"Well, you are. And I'm about to do my best to make both of our fantasies come true."

And Oz began to kiss and nibble her neck, her shoulders, her chest. With deft fingers he unfastened her bra and pushed it off her shoulders, and then took her breasts in his big hands, and then—and then he put his mouth to one of her nipples, rolled it on his tongue, and sucked.

And just like that, she was in heaven. He felt perfect. And she'd been waiting to feel this way for a very long time.

She heard her own panting moans as he lavished attention on one breast, and then the other. He was a careful man, Oz. Careful, meticulous, and thorough. She tangled her fingers in his wild hair, still damp from the snow, and gave herself up to pure sensation.

Oz was in control, now. All she had to do was to trust him. Let her guard down. Be herself, and be proud of her own pleasure, her own desires.

"I can't get enough of your skin," he murmured, kissing a path down her belly, nipping at the top of her underwear and then moving down to stroke her thighs. His chin was just slightly rough with stubble; his lips were gentle, but demanding, and when he took soft nibbles the pressure of his teeth made her cry out. She lifted her bottom to help him slide her panties over her hips.

She felt his breath on her first. And then his tongue: hot, wet, parting her.

Marianne gasped as intense pleasure shot through her. Oz found her clitoris and slowly, carefully, licked her. Small, exquisite, expert circles, each one spiraling her to a new level of excitement. She arched her back, strained toward him, wanting everything he could give her.

"Oz," she pleaded and his caresses became less restrained, though still exquisite, long, sweeping strokes with his tongue and lips. In some forgotten section of her mind she registered that she was clutching the bedspread, thrashing her head back and forth, biting her lip, letting out mewing sounds. Loud sounds. Loud, wonderful, sexy sounds.

And then she felt his finger enter her, slowly, as she'd imagined him doing, and then she lifted her hips off the bed and screamed, throwing her head back into the pillow as her orgasm pounded through her.

He kept touching her. And she kept coming. Great wrenches of pleasure, until she was limp and unaware of anything except for the slow aftershocks.

She opened her eyes. "Wow."

Oz slid up the bed so he was face-to-face with her. "Wow yourself. You were pretty spectacular."

She kissed him and tasted herself on his lips. She ran her hands over his golden skin and hard muscles and she felt her hunger growing again, even stronger knowing what he could do to her.

Oz broke the kiss and rolled half away from her. "Where are you going?" she protested.

"Condoms in the bedside drawer," he answered, reaching for them.

She giggled. "You going to buy Jack a beer tomorrow?"

"I'm hoping I'll get to buy him several."

And he was back in her arms again, filling his hands with her, thrilling her again with passionate kisses on her neck, her breasts, her face. She could feel the hot base of his erection between her legs where she was desperate for him.

"I want you inside me," she told him. "I want you to be wild. I want you to let go."

He made a guttural, carnal sound in his throat and kissed her, so fiercely it took her breath away. He rolled her on her back, wrapped her legs around his waist, grabbed both of her hands and stretched them up over her head so that her body arched into his. Then he thrust into her, a single, hard push, at once so forceful and so wonderful that she cried out again.

"Marianne," she heard him rasp. "You feel amazing."

He was big. Even bigger than he'd felt in her mouth. She felt stretched, full, complete, and so aroused that even with him not moving, buried in her to the hilt, she felt the contractions of another orgasm starting.

"More," she said, and he began moving. Fast, and hard, and deep. He let go of her hands and grabbed hold of her hips to tilt her, plunging even deeper. She dug her fingers into his shoulder and gasped out her pleasure to the rhythm of his movements.

She saw his jaw clench. Sweat was on his forehead, his eyes glazed in ecstasy. But he was with her all the way. Their bodies worked together, as they had on the motorcycle.

"Ride me," he growled and rolled them over so she straddled him with him still inside her. His hands on her hips guided her, fast, up and down on him as he thrust up into her, his muscles clenching under her hands. Frantic. Greedy. Wild and reckless, and growing wilder by the second.

In the midst of their frenzy, she looked into Oz's face and saw him smiling at her. His hair was wet with snow and sweat. His breath came in grunts, his pulse pounded visibly in the cords of his neck. And that smile. The one she'd seen across a crowded room, and recognized right away.

It sent her over the edge again. "Oz," she said, not a scream this time, just a quiet assertion of his name, and she shuddered and convulsed around him.

His hands tightened on her hips, and with a roar and final, mighty thrust he exploded, too.

Marianne collapsed on top of him and he held her tight. Her breathing, like his, was ragged, and her pure skin had a fine sheen of sweat. He was still inside her; he could feel the contractions of her subsiding orgasm.

He loved her.

He kissed her damp forehead and let his chin rest on the top of her head as their hearts beat together.

Now that he knew, it was so simple and easy to understand. Everything he'd been feeling, all the supposedly irrational actions he'd taken: they were all because he was in love with Marianne. Because he'd been in love with her from the moment he'd seen her.

"That was incredible," he heard her murmur against his neck.

"The most incredible thing I've ever done," he agreed.

Life-changing, in fact.

"Let's do it again," she said.

"Aren't you satisfied?"

"I'm more than satisfied. I want to be more than satisfied some more."

"I haven't even caught my breath from the last time," he said, and the action of his laughing made her breasts press harder against his chest. He let his hand wander down to her bottom. "Give me five minutes."

She lifted her head and looked at him. Her face was flushed and there was a sparkle in her blue eyes. "Four minutes."

"Marianne, give me a break here. You drag me away from my very important work, make me go out in the freezing cold, hit me in the head with an iceball, throw me into a snowbank, then tear off my clothes and completely ravish me. I need a little recovery time."

She dimpled, and squeezed him with her inner muscles. Tight, sweet, and exciting.

"Okay, two minutes," he said.

He held her hips to his and rolled them both over, still joined. Propped up on his arms, he could see her more completely. She was exquisite. And clever, and fun. Dignified, ladylike and, in bed, completely abandoned.

The thought engendered a definite stirring in his loins.

"Maybe one minute," he amended. "And another condom."

She made a small bereft sound as he slipped away from her, but then he was back. He dipped his head to begin what he intended to be a thorough process of exploring her skin with his mouth. Starting with the hollow of her left shoulder.

His mind, all the time, was busy exploring this new

idea. He'd fallen in love. At first sight, as Jack had predicted he would. He'd taken so long to recognize it because he hadn't believed that it was possible to have a deep emotional connection with somebody you hardly knew. Especially somebody who refused to tell you about herself or anything about her past.

And because he knew that Marianne was, in all likelihood, probably going to leave Portland.

He stopped, mid-lick on her collarbone.

Marianne, who had been running her hands in the most provocative way down his back and over his backside, paused.

"Oz? Something wrong?"

He looked at her. Her face was even more beautiful now that he knew how precious she was to him.

He shook his head. "Everything's wonderful," he said and kissed her lips.

She'd said it herself: what they were sharing was incredible. It wasn't something that you walked away from. Okay, she had some issues about her past. But they'd work them out together. He'd take it slow, and learn about her, and he'd show her she could trust him.

Her mouth parted and he met her greedy little tongue with his own. Her hands on his buttocks were kneading, pulling him still closer to her, and she was making those soft pleading sounds that drove him crazy.

And he found he didn't need any more recovery time.

He rested on one elbow and used his other hand to caress her breasts as he entered her again. Slow and gentle, this time. He pulled himself nearly out of her, and then, fraction by delicious fraction of an inch, sheathed himself in her again. Again. Again.

He couldn't think anymore, now. He let himself just feel. All the textures of her body, the way she wrapped herself around him and responded to every touch, every stroke. Her voice whispering in his ear urging him on, the sweet friction between them.

Here, in this bed, they were a universe of two.

Her whispers turned to moans, and her hands on him became more urgent. He kept it slow. His fingers teased her nipples, one and then the other. He could feel her climax building in her—extraordinary, he could tell when she was about to come from the tension in her body, the way she held her breath, the thousand little changes in her smell and her temperature and the way she gripped him—and he slowed down even more, so he was barely moving. Just the slightest of pressure into her, more like a tensing than a thrust, and then relaxing for a split second before pressing into her again. They were tiny, tiny movements, and the sensations they produced were like a series of minuscule shocks.

And then her orgasm came, sudden and so intense that it shattered his own control and he followed her, groaning his pleasure into her mouth as she clamped her legs around him, squeezed every little bit of ecstasy from him.

He couldn't hold himself up anymore. He fell to his side on the bed, every muscle in his body exhausted and singing with bliss.

"Gracious," Marianne said, her voice shaky.

He gathered her to him, curled his body around her. "I think you might as well make up your mind to stay here for the rest of the day, and tonight. You won't be able to drive home in this storm. And I have a lot more that I want to do with you." He buried his face in her hair and breathed in her scent. "Stay."

He felt her nodding. “Okay.” She snuggled up to him, all cosy and feminine and more precious than anybody else he’d ever found.

He smiled, and closed his eyes. Everything was going to be fine. Wonderful, in fact.

He had it all figured out.

CHAPTER THIRTEEN

"WHERE'S the world gone?"

Marianne stood at Oz's bedroom window, wearing one of his huge T-shirts, holding a steaming cup of coffee in one hand and buttered toast in the other, and looking out at…nothing.

It must have snowed all night. The entire neighborhood was buried. She could see other houses, and trees, but the rest was snow. There was an indentation where the road should be, and humps of snow that were presumably cars and bushes.

Oz came up behind her and wrapped his arms around her waist. "It's all gone. It's just us."

"Mmm. That sounds good." She finished her toast, put down her coffee, leaned back into the warmth of his body, and enjoyed his hands caressing her through the T-shirt. "I'd like the world to be just you and me. Especially if you keep doing that."

He nuzzled her neck and pressed a kiss to her ear. "I wish it were. Unfortunately I have a lecture to deliver this morning. Without notes, since you distracted me so much yesterday afternoon. And last night. And this morning."

She frowned. "Won't your lecture be canceled with all this snow? The roads are covered."

"This is Maine. Now that it's stopped snowing the plows will have the roads clear in no time."

"I'm going to have to dig out my car to get home." She sighed.

"Hey." He turned her to face him. He was only wearing his underwear, and, even though she'd spent hours looking at him and touching him and tasting him, she still marveled at how beautiful he was. "You don't have to go home. You can stay here, and I'll come back for lunch between my lecture and my afternoon patients."

She shook her head. "No, I told Warren I'd do his accounts for him today. He hates number crunching and I'm good at it."

"Are you?"

Marianne took a split second to think before she nodded. "Uh-huh. I've got an MBA from Duke."

He raised his eyebrows. "Impressive."

"Yeah, we're both ridiculously overeducated." There. She'd told him something about herself, and the world hadn't exploded. Yet.

She kissed him on his chin, and then lightly on his lips. "I'll see you tonight. Come by the bar and I'll give you a beer on the house."

"That's a date." He kissed her again, lingeringly. "You can't drive in this, though, and the plows haven't been yet, so I'll walk you home. If I keep your car hostage here you'll have to come back and spend tonight with me."

"That's a date, too." She pretended to consider. "These dates are free now, aren't they, since I've slept with you? I don't have another three thousand in cash on me."

He laughed. "Free, and frequent, I hope. Do you want any more breakfast before we go? I've got eggs."

She shook her head and pointed to the bed, which was full of crumbs from the breakfast he'd brought them. "I've already had three pieces of toast. Plus, I don't think your rickety kitchen table could take another one of our meals."

They'd wandered downstairs late the night before, hungry and thirsty and needing renewed energy. Oz had made them pasta and salad and they'd just about managed to devour it before their hunger for each other had reasserted itself and they'd been using the kitchen table in all sorts of interesting and athletic ways.

From Oz's expression, and the firmness pressed against her belly, he was remembering it, too. He shook his head as if clearing it.

"Right," he said. "Get dressed, and I'll walk you home. And if you're worried about the kitchen table, tonight we can try the couch."

"Or the bathtub," she suggested, stepping out of his embrace and going to find her clothes.

"This is going to be a really interesting lecture," Oz muttered, tearing his eyes away from her and going into the adjoining bathroom.

"What's it on?" she called above the sound of running water as she pulled on her jeans.

He appeared at the door, razor in hand, face half-covered with shaving foam. "Sex addiction," he answered, and his face was so intelligent and so comically tortured-looking that she ran to kiss him and had her face smeared with shaving foam.

Ten minutes later she was downstairs rinsing the plates they'd neglected last night and stacking them in the dishwasher. Oz appeared in the kitchen, shaven, his hair combed into some semblance of order, and wearing a suit. She abandoned the dishes and whistled, low.

"Who would've thought I'd find a man who looked as good in a suit as in leather chaps and a fake tattoo?" she marveled.

"Hmm, I've got some kinky accessories for you, too." Oz gave her a pair of woollen socks. "Put these on, and then sit down and give me your feet."

The socks were too big, but they'd be much warmer than her cotton ones in the snow. She finished putting them on to see Oz kneeling in front of her on the floor, holding out his hand. She gave him her foot, and he pulled a plastic bread bag on over it.

"What's that?" she yelped.

"I know it's not very stylish, but it'll help keep your feet dry when you're wearing your sneakers." He deftly tucked the leg of her jeans into the bag and tied it around her calf.

"You've done this for all of your younger brothers and sisters, haven't you?"

"Yup." He nodded, putting her other foot in a second bag. "With six of us, someone was always growing out of their boots."

"You're going to be a great dad some day."

She'd said it lightly, without thinking, but when he looked up at her his face was suddenly full of so much longing and hope that she felt her smile melting away.

He looked back down at her foot and finished bagging it. "Okay," he said, standing and giving her a swift kiss on the top of her head, "just put on your sneakers and you can wear my coat and gloves and hat, and you should be fine."

Of course the man wanted children. He'd grown up

in a big family. He had this huge house, way too big for a bachelor.

She followed him into the front hall, her bagged feet making crinkling sounds the whole way, and accepted his big coat and a hat. She watched him tuck the bottoms of his suit trousers into a pair of heavy boots and put on his leather jacket and a thick woollen hat.

"Maine fashion," he said, smiling broadly and picking up a rucksack on their way out of the house.

As they walked he took her hand in his. Their gloves were too thick for her to feel anything, but it steadied her—it was hard to walk in nearly a foot of snow. When they got to the road it was easier; it had obviously been plowed at some point during the night, because the snow was much less deep.

Everything sounded muffled by the snow, even her feet crinkling and their voices as they talked. The sky was clear and bright blue now, and the sunlight on the white snow dazzled her eyes.

It was too bright. She had to keep squinting. His hat was too big, and kept slipping down over her eyes. And even though it was cold, walking through the snow was such hard work that within ten minutes she was sweating inside his huge warm coat.

And any minute she expected him to start talking about what had happened in the kitchen. The fact that he was dying for a permanent relationship and a family. He'd said as much that day in the wedding dress shop.

Somehow, that thought made her feel as stifled as his big heavy coat.

"Tell me about your lecture," she said. She was interested, but she knew she was asking more for a distraction than because she wanted to know about sex addiction.

Oz launched into it with enthusiasm. He was a good teacher: he didn't talk down to her, but he explained the clinical points of addiction to her in a way that she could understand, even without a degree in psychology.

Of course, she'd had some practical experience of compulsive behavior patterns.

The thought made her grit her teeth. She struggled over another snowdrift, trying to ignore how, with the woollen socks and the plastic bags, her sneakers pinched her feet.

"But," Oz continued, stepping with ease over the drift she'd just waded through, "I've decided I'm going to cut down on my lecturing. I'll see the head of department this morning to talk about it."

"Why?" she asked. "Sounds like you love it."

A snowplow passed them: a big, lumbering truck with blades on the front. It shoved the snow out of its way and scattered salt and sand behind it like the excretions of some unnatural animal. It was too loud for them to hear each other, but when it passed they could walk on the plowed road.

"I'm going to stop taking new patients for a while, too," he said. "Until I clear my books a little. I've been working too hard. I need some time to play."

He stopped in the road and pulled her to him and kissed her. When they broke apart, he was smiling ear to ear.

"You look happy," she said.

Why wasn't she?

"I am," he said, taking her hand again. "I think that I've finally got it all figured out."

"That must be nice."

He didn't appear to catch the slight sarcasm in her tone. She was glad he hadn't. He was so happy, full of smiles and energy and affectionate touches. There was no reason she should spoil his good mood just because she was hot and sweaty and feeling a little freaked out by the idea that he might be hoping for a family. With her.

And children were…she swallowed. Children were wonderful. Oz's children would be even more wonderful. But it was so fast.

They reached the bar, and Oz walked her through the alley to her door. "Well, thanks for walking me home," she said, fishing her keys out of her jeans pocket and going to open the door. "I'll see you later I gue—"

The door swung open without her putting her key in the lock.

She frowned.

"Did you leave it unlocked yesterday?" Oz asked behind her.

"It normally shuts and locks itself," she said. "Maybe I didn't shut it hard enough."

Oz moved her out of the way and went up the stairs in front of her.

Her apartment door was wide open.

"Stay here," Oz said, and went into the apartment. She stood in the doorway and looked inside.

Her chair was broken. That was the first thing she saw. There was only one chair in the apartment, and it'd been tipped over and one of the legs was snapped off.

I'll have to sit on the bed, she thought, and then she saw everything else: the plates and teacups smashed on the floor, her neatly folded clothes strewn over her now-unmade bed, her suitcase overturned, even the avocado refrigerator open, with a quart of milk lying empty in front of it like the discarded shell of an insect.

* * *

After the police car dropped them off, they walked up the snowy path to Oz's front door in silence. He carried her suitcase for her. As soon as they got inside she pulled off his huge jacket and sat on the floor to take off her sneakers and untie the plastic bags from around her feet.

"Are you okay?" Oz asked her, hanging up their coats.

"I could have stayed at the apartment," she said. Not looking at him. Not sure why she wasn't looking at him. Not sure why she hadn't felt comfortable all morning and why she was so irritated with Oz.

He'd done everything right. He'd held her during the first shock of realizing her apartment had been broken into. Walked around the apartment, checking the burglar was gone, cataloging the damage, swearing under his breath at the person who'd done this to her. Then he'd called the police, all of whom he seemed to know personally, and sat beside her on the bed with his arm around her shoulders once they'd showed up and started asking her questions. Before they left he'd helped her refold her clothes, mop up the milk, and sweep up the broken dishes. He even managed to screw the leg back on the chair.

He'd been a rock: utterly supportive, sympathetic, and chivalrous. He'd canceled his lecture and he'd absolutely insisted she come back to his house to stay.

She shouldn't be irritated with Oz. She should be irritated with the person who'd broken into her apartment and tossed her stuff around and made her feel as if she'd been somehow violated.

But she was irritated with Oz anyway.

"Your apartment isn't safe," he was saying now. "The

doors were broken. Anybody could walk in from the street. The burglar could come back."

"Why would the burglar come back? I don't have anything to steal, and he knows that now." Her cell phone, her laptop, her expensive jewelry and all her other rich-girl executive possessions had been left behind in Webb.

"I think if he were after money, he'd have broken into the bar instead of your apartment." Oz's voice was grim.

"Don't be silly." She stood up, balling the bags in her hand, and walked past him toward the kitchen.

"I'm being realistic," he said, following her. "You're a beautiful woman. There are a lot of male customers at that bar, and any of them could've seen you going up to your apartment after work." He opened a canister of coffee and started measuring it into the machine. "You'll be safer here, at least until your door is repaired. And I'm not so sure how safe that place is, anyway."

"I don't want any coffee," she snapped.

He shrugged. "Okay. I do." He sat down at the table.

She stayed standing. "I could have gone to stay at Warren's condo. He's my cousin. We look out for each other."

"Warren's at the bar; you'd have to be alone."

"Well, you have to work too. Don't you have patients this afternoon?"

"I'll cancel them. You need someone to be with you. You're obviously upset."

Her irritation was heating from a slow simmer to a full-fledged boil.

"I'm not upset. And I'm going to work tonight anyway, so really there isn't much point in my hanging around here all afternoon."

Oz stood and came to her. He caressed her cheek with his thumb. "Are you sure you should go back to the bar?" He stroked a lock of her hair back behind her ear. "I think maybe you should take a couple days off, stay away until they've found out who did it."

She flinched. "You're acting just like my father, dammit!"

Marianne realized what she'd just said. She put her hand to her mouth, feeling the blood draining from her face.

So that was it.

Oz stepped forward. "Marianne. You just swore. Why are you so angry?" He touched her arm.

Shock at herself turned to fury at him. She wrenched away from him, heat rushing through her body.

"Leave me alone," she said. "Stop controlling me. Stop analyzing me. Stop trying to make me fit into some little box shaped like the perfect woman. Just—stop."

Oz had gone very still.

"Is that how you feel about me?" he asked.

"Yes." She couldn't seem to catch her breath. She was stifled, too hot, too full of anger.

"You think I'm trying to control you? You think that's what this relationship has been about?"

"Yes. But don't think you're special. I feel that way about a lot of people."

He ran his hands through his hair. "I was trying to help you and to understand you. Not to control you." His normally calm voice had an edge to it; he was enunciating his words very clearly.

"It's all the same thing," she said.

"No!"

Marianne jumped; she'd never heard that tone in Oz's voice before. Harsh. Low. Angry.

She'd explored every inch of Oz with her hands and her mouth. But he'd never seemed so strong, such a presence. Not threatening in his anger, not physically dangerous. But—big. Overwhelming.

She took another step back.

"It's not the same thing, Marianne," he said, his hazel eyes blazing. "I care about you. I don't need to order you around. I don't do power games like that. And I'm sorry for whatever has happened to you in your past, but it is not my fault."

"I—"

"And before you tell me to go away, you need to stop blaming me every time you find out something about yourself that you don't like."

"It must feel really good for you to have me all figured out," she said, her voice dripping with fake sweetness. She turned on her heel, walked out of the kitchen, through the hallway, and out the door without bothering to put on her shoes. She slammed his front door behind her and leaned on the porch railing, breathing in the frosty air. The cold was almost painful. It was a relief.

Dammit, she thought, holding on to the word and all it represented. *Dammit, dammit, dammit.*

She heard the door open. Oz stood on the porch beside her. He looked at her feet in the snow in only socks and he didn't say anything, just clunked down the stairs in his heavy boots and waded through the snow to the garage. He opened the door, disappeared inside, and within thirty seconds had come out with a shovel.

He came up on the porch and held the shovel out to

her. "Here," he said. "This is to dig out your car. I assume you don't want any help."

She took the shovel. He stomped the snow off his boots and went back inside.

She got the point. Oh, yes. He wasn't going to help her do anything in case she accused him of trying to manipulate her again.

Marianne opened the door. Thankfully, Oz wasn't in the hallway. She shoved on her sneakers and grabbed her suitcase, and went down the front path to where her car was buried in snow.

"Good," she muttered, leaving her suitcase in a drift and starting to shovel the snow from the front wheels. She didn't need his help. She didn't need anything from anybody. She'd come to Maine, and she'd started her new life, and she could be whoever she wanted to be, and she was free. With every thought, she dug out a shovelful of snow and hurled it back over her shoulder.

She was strong. She was smart. She could do it alone.

The weather had warmed up a little, and the snow was no longer the feathery ice crystals that had been so magical yesterday. It was heavy and wet. It quickly soaked through her sneakers and seeped into her socks, chilling her feet.

"Don't care," she told the snow. "Do what you want, I don't care."

Thing was, she did.

She did care. She wouldn't be so angry if she didn't. Oz was right, darn him.

She stopped and glanced at Oz's house. There was no sign of him.

Good. She didn't need to see him gloating.

She started digging again. The heavy snow made

her arms ache. The handle of the shovel was wood, and it rasped against her cold fingers.

She cared about Oz. And the minute she started caring for anybody, she started thinking she should please them.

That was how she'd lost herself—so badly she'd tried to starve herself. By trying to please her parents, her fiancé, and the whole town of Webb. And when she'd saved herself from that, she'd tried running away to Maine and becoming someone else. Which was just another version of losing herself.

She couldn't do it again.

With a grunt, she scooped away the last of the snow around her car. She opened the trunk and threw in her suitcase. Then she got in her car and turned the heater up high.

She had to sit and warm up for several minutes before she could bring herself to start driving. And…she didn't want to leave Oz's house. She'd been happy here, for the first time in years.

And then, as usual, she'd messed it up.

She put the car in drive with a vehement jerk of her arm, and she hit the gas. The tires slipped a little on the snow, and then she was driving away.

Oz sat back in his office chair and sighed as the door closed after his last appointment.

His afternoon had been packed with client after client. But he wasn't sure what good he'd done them. His work had always been a useful distraction from his life, but it seemed as if that strategy wasn't working anymore since he'd met Marianne.

He'd completely drifted away when talking to Marie

Dunn, his three forty-five appointment. Okay, the woman could talk about nothing for hours, but it was his job, after all, to listen. And he'd found himself arguing with Andy Lucia, his patient who was trying to overcome passive-aggressive behavior patterns.

Basically, he was losing it.

What was he doing? Why had he lost his temper with Marianne? The woman had problems with people trying to control her, and he'd dealt with it by getting angry and throwing a shovel at her?

This is not the way you deal with accusations of being manipulative, Oscar.

He sank his head into his hands.

He'd gotten angry because he'd thought she was being unfair. But now, after seeing patients all afternoon, he wondered if she was right.

What if he was trying to manipulate her? What if he'd chosen this profession because it allowed him to analyze people, change their lives? Because it gave him power?

Tanya, his receptionist, poked her blonde head around his door. "Oz, there's this guy here who says he needs to see you. He's been waiting for half an hour while you were with Miss Coady." She rolled her eyes. "He hasn't been very patient."

"What does he want?"

"Wouldn't say. Said it was personal. Wouldn't tell me his name, either. Do you want to see him, or should I tell him you're busy?"

Oz sighed again. He could probably use all the distraction he could get. "I'll see him."

The man who walked into his office a few minutes later had glossy dark hair streaked with gray. He wore a beautifully tailored suit and when Oz stood the man held out a hand that wore a gold signet ring.

"Dr. Strummer," he said, in a deep voice with a strong southern accent. "My name is Robert Webb. I want to talk to you about my daughter, Marianne."

CHAPTER FOURTEEN

FOR a moment Oz froze in surprise, but he recovered quickly. "Mr. Webb. It's an unexpected pleasure." He shook Mr. Webb's hand, noting his firm grip despite his slight build. He was tall, but not as tall as Oz, and wiry. Oz observed Mr. Webb's eyes traveling over him, sizing him up too. The customary dance of two men who had an interest in the same woman.

"Please, sit down," Oz said, returning Mr. Webb's bone-crushing handshake without letting the courteous smile on his face waver. "What can I do for you?"

Mr. Webb let go of his hand at last, but he stayed standing. "It's very simple, Dr. Strummer. I want you to send her home."

Oz gestured toward the comfortable chair across from his own, and used the pause while Mr. Webb finally sat and he took his chair himself to calm the hackles that had risen at Mr. Webb's tone. *Send her home.* As if Marianne were a child.

"That's an interesting request, Mr. Webb. May I ask why you make it?"

"My daughter abandoned her family, her fiancé, and her job. I think it's obvious why she needs to come home."

A bolt of lightning shot straight through to Oz's heart. "Her fiancé?"

Mr. Webb shrugged. "She broke off their engagement before she left, but it's clear that she hadn't been herself for some time." He looked narrowly at Oz. "Don't you know about how she ran away?"

He swallowed, and regained his composure. "Marianne chose not to share the details with me."

"She left out of the blue. No forwarding address, only a note to say she'd gone. She's Assistant Marketing Director at Webb Enterprises, and she left no warning she wouldn't be at work, either. She took off, leaving all her responsibilities and the people she loved behind. It's completely uncharacteristic behavior. As you can imagine, my wife has been worried to death." Mr. Webb made a gesture of disgust. "And she left all that behind to come up here and work in a bar."

"She is an adult. These choices are her own to make."

"She isn't an adult at the moment, Dr. Strummer. She is a very sick little girl." Mr. Webb raised his hand to his forehead, and looked suddenly tired. "Would you believe she never told us about her hospitalization?"

The pain, which had abated somewhat since hearing Marianne wasn't engaged anymore, came back full force and stronger. Oz stood, his heart hammering. Marianne was sick?

"What hospitalization?" he asked.

Mr. Webb looked up at him and shook his head. "I'm afraid, Dr. Strummer, that this secrecy only makes it more plain how sick she is. We didn't know until Jason—that's her fiancé—told us."

Oz was tempted to grab Marianne's father and shake

him. He clenched his fists. "What did he tell you Marianne was hospitalized for?"

"Anorexia. She admitted herself last year. She was on the point of collapse. My poor, poor little girl."

Slowly, Oz unclenched his fists, though he didn't feel any more relaxed. "Marianne doesn't have anorexia."

"Yes, she does. She nearly died."

Nearly died. Oz felt a wave of sympathy and love for Marianne that nearly knocked him over.

She'd had an eating disorder. It fit her pattern exactly: issues with relinquishing control, her capacity for incredible focus and self-discipline. Her habitual suppression of anger. The fear of her own desire she'd manifested when they'd first met.

The fear she'd been brave enough to overcome. With him.

Oh, Marianne, you are amazing, he thought.

Closely followed by, *Oh, Marianne, what have I done?*

He sat back down.

"I've treated many people with eating disorders, Mr. Webb, and, believe me, Marianne no longer has anorexia. Since I've known her she's demonstrated no pathology toward food whatsoever. In fact, she has a healthier attitude toward food than my three sisters, none of whom have eating disorders either."

Mr. Webb sat forward in his chair. "What are you treating her for, then?"

"What—?" Oz suddenly realized what Mr. Webb meant. "Mr. Webb, I'm not Marianne's psychologist."

"You're not?" Marianne's father stood to his full height, putting his hands on his hips and holding back his shoulders. It was the stance of a powerful man, one used to having commands obeyed. "What are you, then?" he asked. "Her lover?"

Oz considered standing, too. Though he was taller than Mr. Webb, and definitely broader, he doubted Marianne's father would become any less aggressive at being reminded of that. He sat back in his chair, and folded his hands in his lap.

"Yes, I am," he said quietly.

"I see." Mr. Webb stared at him for a moment, with Oz levelly returning his gaze. Finally, he took his hands off his hips, as if realizing that intimidation wasn't going to work here.

"Well, Dr. Strummer," he said, "my request remains the same. You need to send her home to us. If you care about Marianne at all, you'll know that. Her mother and I love her."

His voice softened at that, and Oz suddenly felt that he'd underestimated the man. He was probably afraid, finding out his daughter had nearly died. Underneath his bluff and power games, he loved Marianne. And she'd chosen to leave him.

Oz closed his eyes, feeling another wrench of pain. Marianne had accused him of acting just like her father. And in the end, their positions weren't all that different.

"What does Marianne say about going home?" he asked.

Mr. Webb sat down, leaning forward, his elbows on his knees. "She's sick, she needs her family and to be taken care of. Surely you can see that's best for her."

"Wait a minute," Oz said. "If you've spoken with Marianne, why did you come to me? And why did you think I was her psychologist?"

"The private detective I hired to find her found your business card in her apartment," Mr. Webb said.

Oz had been trying to be calm, reasonable, and civilized. He had tried his best to see Mr. Webb's point of view, despite finding the man overbearing, insensitive, and totally out of touch with his daughter's needs. He was Marianne's father, after all, and Oz owed him courtesy and a fair ear. And Oz had already messed up his own life by losing his temper once today.

With a feeling of relief, he decided he could stop restraining himself and get angry.

He stood. "You hired somebody to break into your daughter's home and scare her to death?" he roared.

Mr. Webb leapt out of his chair, too. "We were terrified, her mother and I! We love her and would do anything to get her back!"

"Try listening to her!" he snapped, and then he remembered, with a sharpness that turned some of his anger into nausea, that he'd tried listening to her in the best way he knew how, and that hadn't worked either.

"Mr. Webb," he said, his voice lower now, "I love your daughter, too. One day, I would like to be your son-in-law. But right now, I am very angry with you. And I would like you please to leave my office."

He held Marianne's father's eyes with his own. They were blue, but lighter than Marianne's. There was such a lot about her that he didn't know, he thought. So much that she'd chosen to hide from him. Just as she'd hidden from this man.

It was a long moment before Mr. Webb nodded curtly. "Fine," he said, and turned and walked out of Oz's office.

It didn't feel like any kind of a victory whatsoever.

Tanya appeared in his office door again. "Oz, are you all right? I thought I heard you shouting."

"I'm fine," he lied.

"No, you're not. You were *shouting*. You never shout. Who was that guy?"

"I want to marry his daughter."

"Oh." She bit her lip. "Wedding plans not going so well, huh?"

"I don't think there's going to be a wedding." He snagged his car keys from his desk. "Can you close up, T? I've got to go see somebody."

"Go get 'er, big guy," Tanya said.

Marianne put down the phone and replaced her credit card in her wallet.

"You're going back."

She jumped at the quiet voice, and then saw Warren, leaning in the broken doorway, watching her. She hadn't heard him coming up the stairs. He walked into the apartment and put his hands on her shoulders.

"I thought you were starting a new life, Marianne," he said.

"I am."

"So why did I just hear you booking a one-way plane ticket to South Carolina?"

"Because I belong in Webb. Just like you said I did. If I'm going to find out who I am, I need to be there."

"When you first got here you said that you couldn't be yourself in Webb. You said everybody had too many expectations of you."

Marianne sighed and sat down on the bed. "It wasn't Webb. It was me. I never learned how to stick up for myself and tell people what I wanted. And if I can't do that there, I'll never be able to do it anywhere."

Warren sat down next to her. His forehead was creased, his handsome face worried. "Marianne, I—are you sure you want to do this?"

"No. I don't want to do this." And that was an understatement. Every inch of her body was full of pain. Every particle of her heart and her mind wanted to go back to this morning, when it had been her and Oz in a big, blank world. No obligations, no plans, no expectations. Just touching and smiling and sharing, and the two of them together.

But that couldn't happen. You didn't get a blank template to do your life over. It was already written, and all you could do was make sure that what came next was the right thing.

"I don't want to do it, but I have to," she said firmly.

"And what about Oz? I thought you two were getting close."

"Oz doesn't want me. He doesn't know who I am. He's lonely since his sister left, and he wants somebody to fill that space. He'll find somebody else."

"And you're going to go to Webb and let him find somebody else?"

Oz with somebody else. The thought hurt so much that she had to start moving, had to get up and start folding the rest of her clothing so she could pack it.

"I tried it up here in Maine," she said, folding a sweater into a precise square. "It didn't work. I need to go back to Webb and sort out my relationships with the people who love me."

His frown had gotten deeper. He shifted on the bed,

clearly uncomfortable. "Uh, cuz, I—I think maybe I need to tell you something."

Concern lanced through her. Warren was always so light, so easygoing and jokey, but now he sounded very serious. "What?"

"I never told you how I left Webb."

"How?"

Warren sighed, and sat back cross-legged on the bed, his back against the wall. "I had a boyfriend in high school. He wasn't from Webb; he was from about twenty miles down the road and we used to meet up in secret. Anyway. We were seen." He shrugged. "So I got a call from your father to visit him at his office. I didn't know what it was at the time, I thought he was going to offer me a summer job or talk about my college applications."

Marianne frowned. "But you didn't go to college."

"No. Uncle Robert—" Warren shook his head. "Oh, Marianne, hon, I really never meant to tell you this. But if you're going back home, you need to know."

"What?" she asked with growing foreboding.

"Your father told me I'd been seen with my boyfriend. And he reminded me of my responsibilities as a Webb. And he reminded me that my father's inheritance had run out years before, and he'd been supporting me and my mother. And he mentioned that as he was intending to pay for my college education, perhaps I could learn to behave as I was supposed to. Or if I couldn't, perhaps I could choose to go to a college on the other side of the country, and decide to stay out there afterward."

She blinked. She didn't know what to say.

"So I told him I didn't want his money, and I graduated high school and left for New York."

"He never told me. You never told me."

"I—"

She frowned. "Warren, why didn't you tell me?"

He looked down at the bedspread. "Your father told me that the main reason he wanted me to go was because I was a bad influence on you. I thought—"

Anger rose in Marianne. She was beginning to recognize the feeling. "You thought he'd driven you away because of me." And added to the anger, this time, was guilt. "He *did* drive you away because of me. Warren, I am so, so sorry."

Warren took Marianne's hand in his. "Hon, I knew that it wasn't your fault as soon as you wrote to me. I got over it. Your father loves you, and he wanted the best for you. I can't blame him for that."

She stared at him, her guts churning with so much emotion she felt as if she was going to be sick. "Warren, if driving people away is how you're supposed to show love, I think I can do without it."

She got up and began gathering what was left of her things.

He was probably going to get another speeding ticket. And another speeding ticket this year could cost him his license.

Who cared?

He put his foot on the gas and screeched away from his office toward the bar. The tires of his car sent up a shower of salt, sand, and melting snow behind them.

As he drove he planned out what he was going to say.

He would not lose his temper. He would stay rational. He would tell her he was sorry that he'd come across as overprotective and controlling. He would reassure her that he respected her ability to make her own decisions and live her own life.

He'd tell her, calmly, that her father had come to see him and told him about her eating disorder. He wasn't sure how she'd react to that, but he couldn't hide the truth from her. He would try to convey how much he admired her for having overcome something like that. And he would say that her father had asked him to encourage her to go home.

That was all he would say. He wouldn't advise her. He wouldn't tell her about the depth of his own feelings. Both of those would put pressure on her.

If she asked his advice, however…

He stopped for a light and scowled.

Absolutely everything pointed to the conclusion that Marianne had unresolved issues awaiting her at home. And Oz knew from all of his clinical training that if a person wanted to move on and change, sooner or later she would have to deal with her past, and particularly with her family.

The light turned green. He turned into the road where the bar was.

Okay. Calm. No pressure. He would be polite about her father. No mention of his own emotions. And if—and only if—she asked, he would give her his opinion that she should consider returning to South Carolina. Despite the fact that he desperately didn't want her to.

It was the logical, rational, most effective approach.

"I can do this," he said aloud, and then slammed on the brakes.

A taxi waited outside the bar, its engine running. And Marianne was at the door, just closing it behind her, her suitcase in her hand.

She was going away. She was leaving him.

His Honda stalled as he leapt out of it, leaving the keys in the ignition. He ran the slippery few yards past the taxi and up the sidewalk to the bar. And then he grabbed Marianne's shoulders, and pulled her into his arms, and gasped, "Don't go, Marianne."

For a moment she was warm and pliant in his embrace. Then she pushed away. "I've got a flight to Charleston in an hour. You told me yourself, Oz, people can't run away from their problems. I'm no better here than I was in South Carolina. I'm going back to sort things out, like I should've done in the first place."

"I was wrong." The words poured out of him, without him knowing what he was saying. "It's different with you. Stay here with me. We'll work through things together."

She shook her head. There was sadness in her smile; he couldn't tell if it was for herself, or if it was pity for him. "I can't, Oz. I have to work through things myself." She started down the sidewalk.

He'd be alone again, and he'd only just found her.

He couldn't think. For once in his life, he only had his emotions to lead him.

"Marianne!" He caught up with her, and ran in front of her so she had to look at him. "I know about your past. Your illness."

She blinked, and he saw a flicker of fear cross her face before it hardened into a suspicion that made his heart ache. "How did you find out?"

"Your father came to my office this afternoon."

"So he knows too." She held her chin up. "Well, good. I'm sick of keeping secrets. Did you call him?"

He was blowing it. Again. "No, believe me, I didn't."

"He got in touch with you, then. I'm glad the two of

you enjoyed discussing me and how sick I am." She picked up her suitcase again and started down the path.

She thought— Oz struggled to think straight, to put this into some logical order, so he could refute her beliefs, explain himself, say anything, *anything,* that would make her stay.

It wasn't there. It was all chaos churning inside his head and his heart. He'd had a plan. What was the plan? Had he messed it up already?

"Marianne," he called after her. Heart pounding, breathless, dizzy with desperation, for the first time in his life he threw every caution to the wind. "I love you."

When she turned around her face was pale, drawn, and distant.

"Goodbye, Oz," she said, and got into the cab.

CHAPTER FIFTEEN

THEY were watching every mouthful Marianne ate.

She tried an experiment. She put a piece of roast beef on her fork and raised it to her mouth, and then put it back down on her plate without eating it.

A worried line appeared between her mother's eyebrows.

She picked up the piece of beef again and, instead of bringing it to her mouth, she waved it slowly back and forth over her plate.

Her father's eyes followed it.

She'd been home three days, and her parents had invited her over every night for dinner. She'd gone back to work the day before, and her father had insisted on taking her out for lunch. At first, she'd thought it was because they were glad to see her that they watched her so closely. Then she'd realized they were counting every calorie she ingested.

She sighed and put her fork down. "Mama, Daddy, I'm not anorexic anymore. I eat like a normal person. You can stop staring at me."

Her father put his own fork down. "I don't mean to stare at you. But your mother and I don't know what to do."

"You're like a stranger," her mother added.

Marianne looked at her parents, the two people she'd known all her life. Her mother was thin, elegant, perfectly dressed and made up; her father was power-suited and his hair was turning gray. They looked the same, but different—as if they'd somehow gotten smaller in the three weeks she'd been in Maine.

She'd spent the taxi ride to the Portland airport forcing herself not to think about Oz. How he'd looked on the sidewalk as she drove away, his words ringing in her ears. "I love you," he'd said.

I love you.

The very idea was too huge to even think about.

So instead she'd thought about what Warren had told her. And by the time she'd walked into the airport and seen her father sitting in the passenger lounge reading a book, waiting for the same flight she was going to take, steam had practically been coming out of her ears.

She hadn't even greeted him. She'd stood in front of him with her fists clenched. "You sent Warren away," she accused.

He looked up from his book, and slowly took his reading glasses off and laid them on the arm of his chair.

"I know," he said. "I was only trying to do what was best for you. But I failed."

And as he said that, for the first time in her life, she saw her father as a man who made mistakes. Who didn't have an immovable master plan for life; who was making it up as he went along, just as she was.

He was just a person. Her mother was just a person. And the town of Webb was made up of people. None of them could force her into a perfect box unless she let them. And it had always been that way. She'd just been too busy cramming herself into her box to see it.

Now, at her parents' dinner table, she watched her mother's face crumple.

"Did we make you sick?" she asked, her voice choked. "Why didn't you tell us? Did we do something wrong?"

Dinner at her house had always been a time to have good manners and talk about school or work or a planned event. Not about emotions.

And it would be easy to blame her parents for that. Or to blame the whole town of Webb and generations of fine breeding.

But she knew, now, that being perfect had been a way of avoiding her own feelings. Never feeling angry, or frightened, or passionate.

She reached over the table and took her mother's hand in hers. "It's all in the past," she said gently. "I'm all right now. And it taught me that I can love you, and not try to be perfect. I can be myself."

Wait. Getting over her illness had taught her how strong she was. It had taught her that she needed to value herself. But it wasn't recovering from anorexia that had taught her that she could *be* herself.

It was Oz who had taught her that.

She swallowed a lump in her own throat.

"Oscar told me that you were healthy now," her father said. "But we only found out recently that you'd ever been sick, so we're still worried about you."

What her father had said didn't filter through right away. When it did, she turned to face him.

"Oscar?" she said. "Oz told you I was healthy?"

Her father nodded. "We had a very illuminating talk. He's a good man, your Oscar. A strong man."

What a surprise. She'd known that her parents would like Oz as soon as she'd seen the "Dr." on his gold card.

"He's very successful," she said dully.

"He knows his own mind. And I have him to thank that you're back here with us."

She frowned. "What do you mean?"

"When I talked with him he flat-out refused to tell you to come back home. But he convinced you in the end, didn't he?"

"No," she said. "Oz didn't tell me to come home. He begged me to stay with him. I decided to come home myself."

Her father nodded. "Oscar told me that you were old enough to make your own decisions. And he was right. That's why I was going back to South Carolina without seeing you."

Without warning, her eyes filled with tears.

She was remembering a room full of wedding dresses, every one of them waiting for a lucky woman to wear them and fill them full of her love. And Oz saying, "I think people should be allowed to make mistakes, don't you?"

What horrible mistake had she made leaving him?

She'd thought she was a substitute for his sister, just a body to fill his loneliness. But he'd never begged his sister to come back. He'd never invited anybody else to fill his loneliness.

She'd thought he was trying to control her, when he'd never done anything but try to set her free.

"Mama, Daddy," she said, squeezing her mother's hand, "I've made a decision I hope you won't be too upset about."

* * *

Through the fog of sleep he could hear his phone ringing.

Oz opened his eyes. The world was totally white. He blinked a few times to focus his eyes and realized it was because the stack of paper beside him on the desk had fallen over his head as he slept.

He pushed it aside and sat up, papers drifting to the floor around him. "Place looks like a blizzard hit it," he muttered as reached for the phone.

A blizzard. The word brought it all back: the snow, Marianne lying on top of him, desire in her deep blue eyes.

The fact that she was gone.

He closed his eyes as the familiar pain hit him yet again. Then he gritted his teeth and picked up the phone. No good thinking about it.

"I'm busy," he said into the receiver.

"Yeah, what else is new?" It was Jack. "What are you doing, burying yourself alive in patient cases?"

Oz removed a file from his lap. "I've got a lot of work to do."

He heard Jack sigh in exasperation. "Oscar. The whole idea of falling in love isn't to give up at the first hurdle and throw yourself back into workaholism."

"I seem to recall that when you thought that Kitty would never love you, your very mature first reaction was to go to a bar and try to pick up girls. Which you couldn't even do." He ran his hands through his hair and surveyed his desk. "At least I'm using my heartbreak constructively."

"Yeah. And I seem to recall that when I was heart-broken, you told me to get some knee pads and beg Kitty to come back to me. Why are you still in Maine, working? She's been gone nearly a week. Go after her."

Oz paced through the ruins of his office as he explained the obvious to Jack. "I can't. For one thing, she would see it as my trying to control her, which is why she left in the first place. For another thing, going after her is exactly what her father did, and he's an arrogant jerk. But most importantly, she doesn't love me. So it's pointless." He sank back into his chair, all his energy gone. "I took a risk, Jack. It didn't work. All I got was a broken heart and an expensive motorcycle."

"But—"

His doorbell rang.

"Jack, are you at my front door on your cell phone? Because I really am busy."

"No, it's not me. I'm at home."

Oz walked through his house to the front door. Through his empty, echoing, lonely house.

"It's Marianne," said Jack. "I've got a feeling."

Oz stopped and looked at the phone. Jack claimed to be psychic, because he'd had a dream about Kitty before he'd met her.

"I don't believe in stuff like that," Oz said. "If it's you on the other side of the door, I'm going to punch you in the nose. So you'd better duck."

He opened the door.

It was Marianne.

Seeing him again was like seeing him for the first time: like an electric shock and a drink of cool water, all at once. Except this time, she knew him. And that made this moment so much better, and so much worse.

"Hi," she said. "Can I come in?"

"Um. I thought you—yeah." He stepped back from the door, and for the first time she noticed he had a phone to his ear. "You were right. I'll punch you later," he said into it, and then switched it off and dropped it on a table.

She'd traveled hundreds of miles to be here and now she couldn't think what to say. *I'm sorry* and *I made a mistake* didn't seem to cut it.

Oz looked wary, alert, but somehow rumpled, as if she'd just woken him up. And seeing him again, she felt as if she'd just woken up, too. She could feel every beat of her heart, pounding fast, the blood rushing to her skin, her lips parting, suddenly hungry. She felt alive, in a way she'd been missing since she'd left him.

Of course, she was also scared to death. She'd left Webb behind her again, and this time it was even more of a risk.

Oz cleared his throat. "So, how's South Carolina?"

He was so quiet. She remembered the last time she'd seen him—the agonized expression so stark on his face as she'd driven away. This time she couldn't tell what he was thinking. For the first time since she'd met him, he was guarded.

That's my fault, she thought.

Okay. She'd made a mistake. She'd made them before, and she'd sorted them out. A mistake wasn't the worst thing in the world anymore.

Except when it hurt Oz.

"It's been hard," she told him. "My family aren't happy with some of my decisions. It's scary for them to realize I'm not the perfect little girl they always wanted me to be. I'm all grown-up, and I've got a lot of flaws. And a life of my own." She let out a short laugh. "My father adores you, by the way."

Oz stared. "You're joking. I could have cheerfully strangled him."

"He admires strong men. And women, too." She sighed. "I could have stood up to him years ago, and it would have been okay, in the end. Going back made me realize that they really do love me no matter what. They just don't always show it the right way. Like Daddy coming after me and finding you."

She shook her head. "If he'd let me be, I would've turned up on my own. But he cared too much, and, for Daddy, that means taking control."

"Just like you think I do?"

"No," she said quickly. "No, you don't do that, Oz. That was my own fault. My own fear, that stopped me from trusting you. You're the only person I've ever known who met me with no preconceptions and tried to find out who I really am."

Neither one of them had moved since she'd stepped into the hallway; they stood, four feet apart, facing each other. Every breath Marianne took into her lungs felt heavy, slow, electric with the desire and hope she felt.

Oz moved. For a heartstopping minute she thought he was going to step toward her, but he just put his hands in the pockets of his jeans. "Why did you come back to Maine?" he asked.

"To say I'm sorry for hurting you. And I'm sorry for not trusting you. And I'm sorry for running away from you, when you opened up to me and told me how you felt."

"I wasn't going to tell you," he said, his voice rough. "I had a calm, logical response all worked out, just like I always have. And I threw it away and just—felt. Instead of thinking. For the first time in my life. And you left anyway."

Tears burned in her eyes. "I did exactly what you said I'd do. The whole reason you didn't want to fall in love with me."

"But you had to."

She nodded.

"I knew you did." He rubbed his face, hard, with both hands. "Sometimes I wish I didn't understand you so well."

"I'm glad you do."

He looked at her. She'd driven straight from the airport, and was still wearing her light jacket and thin leather boots. They were perfect for Webb, but too flimsy for Maine.

"Are you going back to Webb?" Oz asked.

"No. I want to make a new start. And do it right, this time. Not playing at being someone I'm not. Just being me. And being with you."

She took a deep breath for courage, and stepped forward, closed the gap between them. She reached up with both hands to frame his face as she looked into it: the sculpted cheekbones, his strong jaw. His precise nose, the smile lines around his gorgeous mouth. And his eyes that had looked right into her from the first moment.

"I love you, too," she said.

She stood up on tiptoe and kissed him. His lips were firm and soft, as wonderful as she remembered. She heard him taking in a long, deep breath through his nose. Inhaling her.

When he let the breath out, she felt the warm air against her cheek, and heard, low in the back of his throat, the quietest of rumbles. A soft moan of pleasure and desire.

Her heart leapt and her ears rang, like the first time

they had kissed. But this time, they weren't on a stage in front of a crowd of people; they were alone, together.

Just the two of them in a brand new world.

And then his arms were around her exactly as they should be. And his mouth opened and his tongue tasted her, and she tangled her hands in his hair and kissed him as hard as she could. She felt his hands on her, pressing her to him, moving from her shoulders to her waist to her backside to slide up her back and then hold her face, cup her breasts, as if they were hungry to hold all of her at once.

And she wanted all of him. Inside her, around her, again and again. For making love and for laughing and for taking risks and understanding. For ever.

When they broke apart, they were both panting.

"I love you," he gasped, kissing her forehead and her face. "I love you and I want to marry you and have children with you and grow old with you. I know that's a lot to ask and we've only known each other for a little while but we can take it as slow as you want, Marianne. Just as long as I can love you."

She smiled at him. Oz, her bad boy and her good man. She put her lips to his ear, feeling his strong body pressing against her, reveling in his arousal. She knew the look on her face was devilish.

"Actually," she whispered, "we can take it as fast as you like."

EPILOGUE

IT WAS the perfect wedding.

The wedding dress was elegant; the bridesmaids wore simple, dark red raw silk. The flowers were exquisitely scented and coordinated, Valentine-red roses and calla lilies. The groom and the ushers wore tailored morning suits with matching red silk cravats.

Of course Marianne had picked it all out herself.

She looked across at Oz. He looked devastatingly handsome in his suit. His hair was combed, but it was still wild. She wanted to wrap her arms around him and kiss him, but it wasn't done at this point in the ceremony. Especially under the eyes of Oz's father, who was conducting it. He was nearly as tall as Oz but was brown-haired, round-shouldered in his black minister's suit. His kind smile was exactly like his son's.

Marianne stood near the altar, Oz's sisters Jennifer and Alice beside her. Michael and Joe stood beside Oz. And with their hands joined, Daisy and Steve stood in front of Oz's father, repeating the words that would make them husband and wife.

She had to blink back tears when they kissed. She glanced over at Oz, and saw him watching her. Smiling.

He took her arm as they walked up the aisle of the church and whispered in her ear. "Come with me. I've got something to show you before we go to the reception."

She nodded, and went along with him as he detoured her away from the guests filing out behind them, into a side room of the church. It was where Oz's mother taught Sunday school, and it was full of miniature chairs and colorful drawings of Noah's Ark.

"That was absolutely beautiful," she said as he pushed the door shut behind them.

"Thanks to you," Oz said. "And your taste in clothes and flowers. And your diplomacy in getting Daisy to talk to my mother and sisters again."

She smiled. "Who would've thought I'd be the paragon of family reconciliations?"

"I would've," Oz said, drawing her to him and putting his arms around her. "You can do anything you want to do."

"You don't still think your sister's getting married too early?" she asked.

He shook his head. "No. She's the happiest I've ever seen her. And I've learned that you can't control how fast you fall in love."

He kissed her, the tender, passionate kiss she'd been dying to share with him through the entire ceremony. When they split apart she knew her eyes were shining.

Oz smiled at her. He tilted his head, as he did when he was thinking and planning something.

Then, suddenly, he swept her up into his arms and carried her to the desk at the front of the room. He put her down on it and kissed her on the forehead.

"I have something to ask you," he said. He knelt down on the floor.

It had been nearly three months and one week since she'd come back from South Carolina to Maine. November eighth, to February fourteenth. All that time spent with Oz, falling deeper in love with him, getting to know his loved ones, starting her brand new life. Taking it slowly. Relatively slowly, for them, anyway.

And every day she'd hoped he'd kneel down before her and ask her something.

"The answer is yes," she said.

He blinked, his face the picture of comic exasperation. "Let me ask before you answer, I've rehearsed this."

"I've been waiting for ages. I was thinking I'd have to get Lizzie to hold a husband auction."

"You are shameless." He reached into the pocket of his morning suit and pulled out a velvet box. The ring nestled in it was a delicate gold band, with a diamond as clear and pure as that first snowfall together.

"Marianne Webb, will you marry me?" Oz asked.

"Yes. Yes, yes, yes, yes, yes. It's what I want more than anything in the world. Put the ring on me."

"I love it when you're a bossy little thing," he said.

He slid it onto her finger.

And then pulled her into his lap and kissed her so long and hard that she lost all track of time.

"Oz," she gasped between kisses, one of his hands stroking her back, the other one underneath her red silk skirt caressing up her bare leg, "there's a limousine waiting to take us to the reception."

"Nope," he said.

"Yes, there is. Daisy asked me to book it."

"Nope," he said again. He stood up, taking her with him, and carried her out of the Sunday school room and across the aisle of the church. "We've got our own transport," he said, and opened the church door.

The Harley stood in the street outside, its red and chrome shining in the clear February sun. Its handlebars were tied with white ribbons.

Marianne laughed. He placed her on the back of the motorcycle and gave her her leather jacket and helmet. She put them on, and hitched up her skirt, and wrapped her legs and her arms around Oz.

"Ready for some foreplay?" he asked, starting the motor and starting that thrilling vibration against her body.

"Always," she said.

Their trip was like flying through the streets of Portland, toward the hotel where the reception was going to be. It was a beautiful hotel, with views of Casco Bay and the Portland Head Light. Marianne had chosen it herself. But at the moment, she didn't want their ride to end. Right now they were the only two people in the world. When they got to the hotel it would be family and friends and Daisy's big day.

One day soon, it would be their day. But for now she hugged Oz tight to her and savored the moments with him.

He pulled up in front of the hotel and she took off her helmet, smoothing her hair back into place. "That's one thing about going fast," she complained. "You get to the place you're going sooner."

"I hope that's not going to be a problem." Oz took her hand as they walked up to the entrance to the white-clapboarded hotel. The outside was festooned with white balloons and streamers, and a pyramid of roses and lilies stood on the porch.

Oz squeezed her hand. And opened the door.

The room was full of people, as she'd expected.

But she hadn't expected the enormous cheer that greeted her.

All the guests, in their wedding finery, held their hands up in the air and clapped, smiled, whooped at them as they walked into the room.

They were cheering for *her.* Her, and Oz.

And Marianne saw people who hadn't been in the church at Daisy's wedding. Lizzie, and the staff of the youth center, where she'd been volunteering since she'd come back to Maine. Some of the teenagers who came there, awkward in their suits.

Warren came forward. He was wearing a morning suit like Oz's, though he hadn't been in Daisy's wedding. He hugged her. "C'mon up here, hon," he said, and took the hand that Oz wasn't holding, and led them both to the front of the room.

And there, standing in front of the floor-to-ceiling windows that overlooked the bay and the Head Light, was Oz's father in his minister's suit. Beside him, Jack in a morning suit, Kitty in a red silk dress like the ones Marianne had picked out for Daisy's bridesmaids. Like the one Marianne was wearing now. Oz's mother, and all of Oz's brothers and sisters, including Daisy and Steve.

And Marianne's mother and father, elegant and impeccable, their eyes brimming with tears. Her mother stepped forward and gave Marianne a bouquet of calla lilies and roses. Just like the one Marianne would have chosen for herself.

"Did I mention that I wanted you to marry me right now?" Oz asked.

Marianne kissed him, to the sound of more applause

from their family and friends. And then, hand in hand, Oz beside her, they stepped forward into the dizzying rush of their future.

0406/171

MILLS & BOON®

Live the emotion

Modern romance™ Extra

Two longer and more passionate stories every month

JUST ONE SPARK…

by Jenna Bayley-Burke

Mason knew Hannah was the one the first time he saw her. Hannah was irresistible, confident, and sexy as hell – but she wouldn't let him give her anything more than mind-blowing sex! Perhaps actions could speak louder than words…

THE PERFECT BOYFRIEND

by Barbara Dunlop

Megan Brock is amazed when her new book on dating causes a storm. And when sexy Collin O'Patrick is offered the chance to put her theories to the test, he is ready for the challenge – Megan obviously doesn't know what she has been missing…

On sale 5th May 2006

Available at WHSmith, Tesco, ASDA, Borders, Eason, Sainsbury's and most bookshops

www.millsandboon.co.uk

0406/01a

MILLS & BOON®
Live the emotion

Modern romance™

THE GREEK'S CHOSEN WIFE by *Lynne Graham*

Prudence and Nikolos Angelis's convenient marriage has never been consummated. But Prudence longs for a baby and must ask Nik for a divorce. He is horrified and insists she stays. Prudence can handle their marriage...but having Nik's child?

JACK RIORDAN'S BABY by *Anne Mather*

Jack Riordan was drop-dead gorgeous and a real man. But he and Rachel had grown so far apart since she had failed to bear him a child. Now Rachel wants to win Jack back. And perhaps, this time, she'll conceive his much wanted baby...

THE SHEIKH'S DISOBEDIENT BRIDE by *Jane Porter*

Sheikh Tair lives by the rules of the desert. When he finds Tally has broken one of those laws, Tair has to act. Tally is kept like a slave girl, and her instinct is to flee – but as ruler, Tair must tame her. He certainly knows he wants her – willing or not!

WIFE AGAINST HER WILL by *Sara Craven*

Darcy Langton is horrified when she is forced to wed arrogant businessman Joel Castille – although she can't resist his sensual persuasions. When Darcy makes a shocking discovery about her husband, it's up to Joel to woo her back...

On sale 5th May 2006

Available at WHSmith, Tesco, ASDA, Borders, Eason, Sainsbury's and most bookshops

www.millsandboon.co.uk

0406/01b

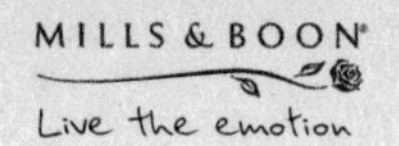

Modern
romance™

BOUGHT FOR THE MARRIAGE BED
by Melanie Milburne

Nina will do anything to keep her twin's baby from harm. So when Marc Marcello wants to take his brother's child, Nina lets herself be bought as Marc's bride instead. But what price can be placed on her...in his bed?

THE ITALIAN'S WEDDING ULTIMATUM
by Kim Lawrence

Alessandro Di Livio always protects his family, even seducing gold digging Sam Maguire to keep her away from his brother-in-law! But when passion leads to pregnancy, Alessandro wants to keep Sam as his wife – and their baby as his heir!

THE INNOCENT VIRGIN *by Carole Mortimer*

Abby Freeman is thrilled when she gets a job as a TV chat show host, and who better to grill than famous journalist Max Harding? Max is happy to let Abby get close – but only in private. How can Abby get the story...without losing her innocence?

RUTHLESS REUNION *by Elizabeth Power*

Sanchia has amnesia but when Alex Sabre recognises her, she realises they once knew each other intimately. To unlock her past Sanchia must spend time with Alex. What happens when she learns the truth about the man she's falling in love with...again?

On sale 5th May 2006

Available at WHSmith, Tesco, ASDA, Borders, Eason, Sainsbury's and most bookshops

www.millsandboon.co.uk

0406/OUEENS/MB020

Queens of Romance

An outstanding collection by international bestselling authors.

17th March 2006

7th April 2006

21st April 2006

5th May 2006

Collect all 4 superb books!

Available at WH Smith, Tesco, ASDA, Borders, Eason, Sainsbury's and all good paperback bookshops

www.millsandboon.co.uk

0506/055/MB033

There's a mystery around every corner...

FOOLING AROUND by Linda Turner

Before inheriting a detective agency, Josie London's only adventures came courtesy of her favourite books. Now she was donning disguises and teaming up with Willey Valentine to trail a mobster.

THE MAN IN THE SHADOWS by Ingrid Weaver

Detective Sloan Morrissey has been missing for a year, but private investigator Erika Balogh is sure she's spotted him on the streets and inhaled his scent in her bedroom. Is her lover still alive?

A MIDSUMMER NIGHT'S MURDER by Julie Miller

When English professor Hannah Greene sets off on a wilderness hike, she doesn't expect people to start dying. To stay alive, she'll have to work with guide Rafe Kincaid and find the killer among them.

On sale 21st April 2006

Available at WHSmith, Tesco, ASDA, Borders, Eason, Sainsbury's and all good paperback bookshops

www.millsandboon.co.uk